From *Flares Amidst Shadows* Productions

忍者、ヒットマン

ASOYA

Shadows From The Past: Part 2

TRANG

ASOYA

Shadows From the Past

(忍者、ヒットマン)

PART 2
TRANG

JOSEPH DAVAULIA

XULON PRESS

Xulon Press
2301 Lucien Way #415
Maitland, FL 32751
407.339.4217
www.xulonpress.com

Unless otherwise indicated, Scripture quotations taken from the King James Version (KJV)–*public domain.*

Paperback ISBN-13: 978-1-6628-3216-1
Ebook ISBN-13: 978-1-6628-3217-8

TABLE OF CONTENTS

忍者、ヒットマン

Section 1

The Hitman, the Word Carrier, and the Almighty

ヒットマン　　　　ワードキャリア　　　　全能者

Ruthless　　　Vermillion

冷酷　　　朱色

CHAPTER 1

SHADOWS AND ITS PHILOSOPHY TO NINJA

THERE ARE MANY DIFFERENT TYPES OF AGENTS throughout the world, but in Japan, there are no agents that are named among the hidden ones that are more lethal or feared then the ninja. It's not the known things about ninja that cause people to fear them, but rather, the unknown, 隠されたもの the hidden things—the shadows. They can strike at a moment's notice, and they are unpredictable. For a ninja, the shadows are a philosophy, a teacher.

Natural shadows are quiet, but even though they don't make a sound, they are there; they move subtly as the person they are following moves. Ninjas are taught to be this exact same way: subtle, undetectable 検出不能, and unnoticed. A shadow is also something that these agents are taught never to escape from. Once a ninja leaves their clan, separating themselves from them, can they ever really escape its shadow?

CHAPTER 2

KOROSHIYA VERMILLION

AS ASOYA WALKS UP A HILL GAZING AT A NEARBY tree, one of the leaves breaks off and floats downward, spinning slowly, making its way down to the grass. The spinning of the leaf reminds Asoya of a shuriken. It was not the leaf itself but the way that it spun; it twirled like a throwing star 投げ星 twirls. This spinning action triggers a memory, causing him to think of when he was a *Koroshiya*, a hitman for the clan, the ninja known as Vermillion.

"Koroshiya Vermillion, the master desires an audience with you," A messenger ninja said, placing his fist in his palm and bowing his head to Vermillion. Vermillion lowered his head in respect, grabbed his sword, and followed the ninja to their master's quarters.

"The shadows are our ally," the messenger said as they made it to the quarter's doors.

4

"They are our allies," Vermillion replied in agreement. The ninja bowed before Vermillion, then sprinted off to deliver messages to other ninjas within the clan. There were two large, muscular ninjas holding axes in their hands, guarding their master's quarters. Vermillion frowned at them; they nodded their heads, then opened the doors, allowing him an audience with their leader. He entered in, and the doors leisurely closed behind him.

"You summoned me, Master."

Vermillion spoke as he walked closer to the area where his master was seated. Vermillion unsheathed his sword; it was newly polished and had a hazy glow to it as the dim candlelight of the room hit it. He gently got on his knees, placing his sword in front of himself. His hand was still on the blade's handle as four of his fingers from his other hand lightly touched the cold steel of his sword as he bowed before his master.

"My sword is at your service."

His master personally issued a mission he wanted Vermillion to undertake. This mission was to take out a man; a government official had paid the clan to silence him because he was causing trouble for the official and those who worked under him. After hearing his assignment, Vermillion looked up.

"What has this man done against you or the clan, Master, that we have been hired to silence him?"

"All you need to know is that he is my enemy," his master said.

Vermillion thought for a moment, then placed his forearm and fist over his own chest and said, "An enemy of my master is an enemy of mine." Vermillion then bowed before his master and picked up his sword that had the words 'dragon smoke' edged deep into its metal. He placed it in his sheath and tied the sheath to his back. He then walked out of his master's quarters and past a ninja with long blue hair, most of which covered the ninja's face; this ninja was also a Koroshiya. The ninja had his back against the wall with his arms folded, and his cased sword was in his hand. When Vermillion walked past him, the ninja moved the hair out of his face and opened his eyes.

"Assume nothing," the ninja said.

Vermillion stopped walking and paused for a moment.

"But be ready for anything."

Vermillion replied as he frowned looking at the ninja. The ninja frowned back as he stared at Vermillion, and then he walked over to Vermillion and placed his hand on Vermillion's shoulder.

"That's right, brother, be ready," the ninja said with a smile, pleased that Vermillion remembered his training.

"A true ninja of the shadows must always be ready, ready for anything," Vermillion said as he took his eyes off the ninja and stared into the distance. Vermillion then walked forwards, and after taking a few steps, he stopped.

"I haven't forgotten what you've taught me, brother," he said. He then lifted the black cloth that was around his neck, covering

6

his nose and mouth as he left for his mission. The ninja walked back over to the wall, propped his back against it, folded his arms, and lowered his head, causing his hair to cover his face once again. He then closed his eyes and spoke, "We are clandestine."

CHAPTER 3

THE WHISPERING OF THE SHADOWS

VERMILLION QUICKLY ARRIVED AT THE GIVEN TAR-get's location that night, for he was eager to fulfill what his master had ordered. Outside of the man's home, Vermillion ruffled the bushes to draw the man out and draw him out he did, for the target walked outside hearing a commotion from the bushes, thinking that it was an animal. Once he was outside, he picked up a stick and walked past a shadow … it was this shadow that Vermillion was hidden in.

The man heard a voice speak from the shadow. The voice said, "Stop walking. Turn around, but do not make a sound."

The man was petrified, for he had heard tales of shadow whispers. If you heard a whisper coming from a shadow, a ninja was upon you. *A ninja!* The man thought, knowing he was in the presence of a mercenary, that his first response should be to run as hard and as fast as he could, but reasoning quickly took over, realizing that such things would not work in the presence of a shadow, in the presence of a ninja 忍者. He quickly dropped the stick he was holding.

"Who are you?" the man asked, as he turned around slowly and in a non-threatening manner, as his voice went up in pitch due to fright.

The voice from the shadow spoke again. "Ruthless. Vermillion." the Koroshiya said still hidden in the shadow, revealing the name he was given in the clan. Vermillion slowly stepped out of the shadows and reached behind his back, where he laid hold on his sword's handle, and after staring at the man with an empty gaze, he unsheathed his sword called 'dragon smoke.'

"Please, you don't have … to … do this," the man said, begging with fear, seeing a ninja with a drawn weapon. The man read the word that was edged deep into the blade, ドラゴンスモーク, then started to shake.

"The enemies of my master are the enemies of me: this is what my master ordered. I am under contract; the law of ninja must be upheld," Vermillion said as he raised his blade above his head. Ruthless Vermillion did what he was taught in the philosophy of ninja to do, to slay 殺す.

The present:

Asoya stops thinking about the time when he was a ninja known as Vermillion. The leaf that Asoya watched spin to the grass was moving lightly, the wind causing the leaf to dance around and then travel a distance away from that location. As he watches the leaf move, he speaks.

"You were right, Word Carrier, everything you told me was correct," he says being thankful that the Word Carrier before him revealed to him the truths of God's word.

"I was doing the work of the dragon but not anymore."

He thinks about how Jesus healed his body from his scars and made him a new person, a person that carries His word; he also thinks about Psalms 91.

"Lord, the Creator of heaven, earth and all living things, you are my Master now," Asoya said looking up from his sheathed sword. "You are my Master. You have been our dwelling place (the dwelling place of those who trust in you) in all generations. Before the mountains were brought forth, or ever, You formed the earth and the world, even from everlasting to everlasting, You *are* God. I will tell others about you and Your Shadow, the shadow of The Almighty."

全能の影 (Ps. 90:1–2).

CHAPTER 4

THE WORD CARRIER NAMED ASOYA

A WORD CARRIER DOES MORE THAN JUST CARRY GOD'S word. They allow it to dwell in them because it is living. Asoya is now a name amongst them who do just that and is a Candle, who, in his former way of living, was a trained shadow 訓練された影. He was brought up from a youth to practice with the art of soundlessness and secrecy; he was taught to be a *Koroshiya*, a ninja, a hitman ヒットマン.

"We are clandestine," his old friend and teacher would often say. He had long since left that life behind himself to walk in the light as it is written in John 1:7, "But if we walk in the light, as he is in the light, we have fellowship one with another, and the blood of Jesus Christ his Son cleanseth us from all sin."

He had been commissioned and given a new mission since walking in the light, to make known God's Word, the Words of Life, and the Words of Truth to the people in his region, leading them in the ways of the Messiah, Jesus, who has become his Master.

CHAPTER 5

THE SHADOW OF THE ALMIGHTY

ASOYA PRAYS FOR A FEW HOURS, AND AFTERWARDS HE was given direction from the word that he was carrying to go into a small village about four hours from where he was staying. He leaves for the small village and upon entering, Asoya immediately knows that he was to bring God's word to the people in that community. That day, Asoya spoke to eight individuals; five received the truth of God's word while the other three did not. He was invited into the home of a family who desires to hear more about the God of Heaven 天の神. He speaks to the family about shadows. Not the shadows that come from one's past, but rather the shadow that comes from above, from the Lord, The Almighty.

"The Almighty has a shadow for us to abide under, and that shadow is his protection. Psalm 91 says that the person who chooses to dwell in the Lord and who makes Him their home and abode, which is in the secret place of the most High, that person shall, without a shadow of a doubt, abide under his protection."

"What is the secret place 秘密の場所?" asks the man as he looks over at his wife and then back at Asoya.

"Is it at some known location or hidden gathering?"

"No," Asoya chuckles, but he does so lightly, knowing why the man would think such a thing. "The secret place is a place you go to personally with the Lord, a place where it is just you and Him. It is you and His relationship. So, one can also say the person who has a personal relationship with the Most High, who abides in Him, and continually makes Him their dwelling place, shall abide under His protection. Do you understand these words?"

The man nods his head as to say yes, and his wife smiles. After showing the man and his wife what was written in Matthew 6:6, and explaining the importance of taking out personal time to spend with the Lord throughout their daily lives, he shows them John 4:21. Once he reads that verse, they understood why Asoya continued to talk about Psalm 91.

"To the person who dwells in Him, Him meaning the Lord and Him meaning the Most High God 全能の神; that person, the one who chooses to dwell in Him shall abide under His shadow, the shadow of the Almighty."

Asoya takes out a piece of paper and drawing utensils to sketch Psalms 91 to give them a physical picture of what it looks like to the person who abides under the Almighty's shadow. After an hour of explaining parts of the chapter, Asoya rolls up the scroll he was reading from and finishes eating the soup the family had prepared for him.

"Do you mind if we keep the drawing?" the man's wife asks.

"Keep the drawing?" Asoya asks, as he thinks for a moment.

"I want to hang it on our wall to remind myself and family to always dwell in the Lord, under the Almighty's shadow," the man says as he and his wife held one another. Asoya smiles, then agrees but only after instructing them not to worship a piece of paper but the actual Lord Himself. Asoya rose from their table and headed for the door where his sword was propped up against the wall.

"How did you come to know so much about those words that you are carrying?" the man asks.

"It's not about carrying the word, but actually allowing His words to abide in you. When a person does this, the Lord gives them understanding on many things," he says as he picks up his sword and throws it over his shoulder, holding it by the string. The children run up and hug Asoya's legs; he pats them on their head and hands each of their children gifts from his travels. He then bows his head to the family, and they all bow back and then rise. He heads out the door. It was now late, and Asoya was preparing to leave the small community. Upon leaving, one of the villagers opens his window and says to Asoya as he was passing by, "There's been a change in the clouds. You might want to take shelter; a storm is coming." With that said, the villager slowly closes his window. As it closes, the sky begins to make thunder and lighting.

"Storms ..." Asoya says as he looks up into the sky. "I welcome them."

He places his Sugegasa hat on his head, tilts it, then pulls up the scarf that was wrapped around his neck over his mouth to stay hidden as he travels during the night. As he walks, the rain began to pour violently, beating hard upon the ground and tapping strongly upon his Sugegasa hat.

保護

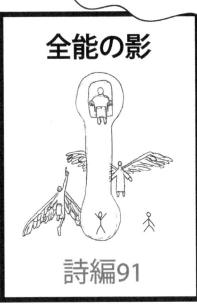

The Almighty/Omnipotent One.

全能の影

詩編91

蝋燭

If you live in God, you will remain under His shadow.

CHAPTER 6

NINJA AND FEALTY

PEOPLE TAKE MANY PATHS WHEN WALKING THROUGH the course of this life; these paths have their own set of rules, their own values, functions and structures. The paths of those who are named amongst the ninja are that of loyalty 献身. By definition, this form of loyalty is allegiance 忠誠; allegiance to their clan, their mission, and above all else, to the will of their master. They are clandestine; anything that opposes this path or if anyone chooses to separate themselves from this way of life that they have sworn by oaths to live, is considered a dissident or is performing a rebel-lion, something that is simply not tolerated in the arena of assassins.

CHAPTER 7

RED VELVET

THERE IS A NINJA WHO IS PART OF THE SAME CLAN

that Asoya separated himself from; this ninja's name is Red Velvet. Asoya, who was titled Ruthless Vermillion, was known as the clan's Gladiator, but Red Velvet … well, Red Velvet was something else entirely. He had no knowledge of Asoya's abandonment 放棄 due to him being assigned deep undercover work in the Northern sector of Japan. A messenger ninja, also known as a spy 間諜, makes his way to Red Velvet's location with the news.

"Does master know that you are here?"

Red Velvet asks as he looks over at a shadow that was cast in the distance. A ninja emerges out of the shadow and kneels before him, showing him the respect due to him being the second highest-ranking member of their clan.

"No, Red Velvet," the messenger replied.

"Good, let us leave it that way, for in this matter, covertness shall be our ally."

"It shall be as you have spoken," the messenger says, lowering his head just a little lower. "What report do you bring me about the well-being of the clan?" asks Red Velvet.

"Master is recovering from a head injury that he sustained from a plank, which dislodged itself and struck him on the head when a fire that broke out."

"A fire?" Red Velvet asks as he turns and looks at the ninja who was still kneeling.

"Yes, Red Velvet, and the clan … the clan its … its main head-quarters has burned down, but it is being rebuilt as we speak and has been relocated."

"Burned down? Was this the work of Gekijō?"

"No, it was not. Shatter was unconscious when this all transpired; he was not behind this."

"Behind this, you speak as though this was a deliberate sabotage," says Red Velvet. "Who would dare to make a challenge against the clan? Answer me right now."

"It was …" the messenger ninja hesitates to speak about who was behind the fire. He scoots himself back, putting some distance between himself and Red Velvet.

"Answer me now, foot soldier! Who reduced our clan to ashes?" Red Velvet asks with agitation but calmness.

The ninja sighs, then looks down at the floor. "It was the Ruthless one."

"Vermillion? 冷酷な朱色 Ruthless Vermillion?"

"Yes, Red Velvet, it was he."

"You lie!" he shouts as he unsheathes his sword and walks towards the ninja in disbelief. The ninja rises and lifts his arms as a form of surrender, showing Red Velvet a scar he sustained from fighting Asoya that day.

"I was there; Ruthless Vermillion gave me this scar on my forearm. He told me not to reach for the signal flair that would have warned the others he was near. I tried, and that is when he struck me."

Red Velvet interrupts. "Vermillion scars no one; he only leaves them lifeless. If it was Vermillion, you would not be alive to tell me this now. You are delusional. You must have been struck on the head by some unknown intruder who has risen in the ranks from our rival clan. No assassin from our own dwelling would dare do such a thing." he says, sheathing his sword, believing the ninja's words to be a farce.

"Delusional? I am not here trying to insult your intelligence but how can eight of our clan members share the same delusion, including Gekijō? It was Vermilion. He is different somehow; he has abandoned our ways. He does not kill any longer."

"He doesn't kill? Dissidence is not tolerated. Vermillion knows this. I shall see if what you speak of is true, and if I find that you have deceived me ..."

Red Velvet takes out two of his gold-plated throwing stars, clanks them together hard three times. Each time they strike against each other, they spark.

"My shurikens shall have their fill of your visage."

The ninja lowers his head and places his fist over his own heart as he leisurely disappears into a shadow. There was no sound to hear within the room; the messenger was gone. Red Velvet follows the law of the assassins without waver. He does not falter. The oaths of the clan must be upheld; they are the law.

"No remorse," he says, looking down at his two shurikens as they shimmer.

CHAPTER 8

THE PONDING RAIN

A MONTH HAS GONE BY; IT IS CLOSE TO THE END OF THE season of Netsu as the summer temperature has dropped marginally. Clouds that have subtle darkness to them have painted the sky once again, and rain is on the horizon. Asoya has spoken to many people about The Almighty and the Almighty's shadow as written in the book of Psalms, specifically Psalm 91. He leaves a village looking down at the scroll with Psalm 91 written upon it; two drops of water tap on the page, then five more, and he looks up at the sky.

"Another storm," he says as he rolls up the scroll, putting it away. He then covers his head with the Sugegasa, and he travels onward. The rain picks up and starts to drop from the sky with intensity. The water is escaping the clouds that hold them and it patters on the leaves, bouncing off the blades of grass before making its way to the soil.

"I heard the speech you gave three towns back to some villagers about shadows. Vermillion, you speak about shadows as though they are past, but surely you can see that they are very near. Have you forgotten about the whispers?" a voice says with power behind it.

"Whispers?" Asoya asks, with a faint smile.

The voice spoke again.

"Once you hear the whispers, you know that a ninja is upon you. Once a ninja has manifested, there is no getting away; there is only *Hametsu*."

By definition, when it comes to ninja, Hametsu means ruin 破滅. The rain beat hard upon the trees and the surrounding rocks, it splashes against the mud and already formed puddles. Asoya was in no temperament to battle with his past self again, for he knew that his past had shown up to slow him down from speaking God's word. He ignores the shadowy figure and walks in another direction, taking a detour, but the shadow did not go away. After thirty-five minutes of walking in the storm, Asoya sees the shadowy figure again ahead of him; it was standing motionless. He could not make out who it was due to the heavy rainfall and the lightning strikes across the sky. Eventually, seeing who it is, Asoya says, "You again? I defeated you once with God's word, and this time will be no different."

CHAPTER 9

THE HITMAN ヒットマン

THE SHADOWY FIGURE JUST SMIRKS UNDERNEATH THE black veil that conceals its mouth and nose.

"I will not allow my past self to have dominion over …" Asoya says as a throwing star is heaved at him as though it were a harpoon. It glides in the air, slicing through the rain. Asoya sees it coming, and his reflexes take over as he lifts his sheathed sword slightly, opening it, pinging off the star without thinking. The star collides against the steel, spinning away from Asoya. It lands in the house beside him, shaking the house lightly. Asoya looks down at his halfway-opened sword due to its ringing, and his hands tingle. He slides it shut, but it continues to ring and both of his hands are still stinging. He looks up at the shadowy figure, then glances over at the star embedded in the house alongside him. The star was plated in gold.

25

"It can't be ..." Asoya says in disbelief, almost falling over as he takes two steps back. The gold-plated star was a trademark for a ninja he once knew, a hitman. He looks at the shadowy figure in the distance. "Trang."

"The clan is like a noose that is tied around your limbs; it tightens its grip the harder you struggle" the shadowy figure says with deep enmity 敵意. The shadow points its star at Asoya.

"Do ... not ... struggle." This command was spoken with fervency. Lighting strikes a second time, but this time it was closer, causing Asoya to see the face of a ninja, whose name was indeed Trang. He, too, was wearing a Sugegasa スゲガサ upon his head. Trang reaches up slowly, tugging on the hat, causing it to be pulled over his eyes.

"That's what daggers are for, to sever ropes, the things that tie too tightly around you," Asoya says frowning, then softens his face.

"Brother, do not fight against me. I am not your enemy."

"Brother? You speak treachery. You understand our ways, what makes us what we are. We are weapons. When an oath has been made to the clan, it must be kept without vacillation, this is the law. You have chosen to turn against your ties, your vows, and you have the GALL to call me brother?!" He shouts as he launches two shurikens at Asoya. They spin with an unquenchable appetite that can only be satisfied once they have landed on Asoya, who speedily lifts his sheathed sword to shield himself from the stars. One of the stars hits his sword, and a numbness shoots from Asoya's wrist all the way up to his elbow. The second star rams into the sheath like a raging rhinoceros. The sheath spins from Asoya's hand, whereby he jumps into the air and catches his sheath, and when his feet touch the damp ground, the blade inside the sheath rings with a high pitched intensity.

Asoya shakes his hand from it temporally going numb, and he looks at Trang. Trang sighs and vaguely tilts the Sugegasa up, looking at Asoya. It is not Asoya that Trang sees, but the ninja from the clan, who is called Vermillion.

CHAPTER 10

THE FEUD OF ABANDONMENT

"BROTHER, YOU SAY, SAVE YOUR WORDS, TRAITOR," Trang says as Asoya lowers his sheathed sword and rubs his own elbow.

"The law," Asoya says, thinking on the law of the clan. "Those who stray must be found and brought back to the fold of assassins; if there is resistance, by oath, severity must be brought upon them with no remorse. The law…" Asoya stumbles in his thought as the sound of rainfall soon overpowers his thinking.

"Your words, they reek … they reek of broken fealty," Trang says as he taps the two throwing stars that were in his hands together four times. Tick … tick … tick …tick. There was a brief period of silence; the rain was speaking for them.

"It took you far too long to identify your pursuer. I am abhorred by your petty insolence, as a ninja, you should never be the one who is crept upon, but be the one doing the creeping," Trang says.

Asoya responds with, "Petty insolence, to call you brother is not insolence, Trang."

"Hold your tongue! You deserted us. You don't have the right to call me by that name. Call me only by my shadow name, the Red Velvet Shuriken," Trang says, taking out a third gold-plated throwing star and looks down at it. Rain bounces off of it as though it were trying to pound it from his grasp, but his grasp tightens. After gazing at it for a while, Trang speaks again.

"The only sound I want to hear at this moment is the clashing of metal that our blades will make when they converse."

Trang frowns and says "Draw out your blade … Ruthless … Vermillion," as though issuing an order to Asoya, who looks down upon the ground and thinks for a moment, then places his eyes back on Trang.

Asoya says, "I'm not the same person I used to be, my heart is now changed. I don't war against flesh and blood."

"Flesh and blood? What do you think we do with these weapons that we carry except war 戦争… now stop speaking vague riddles and draw!"

Asoya sighs, then says, "Okay."

Asoya reached his hand behind himself and pulled out a scroll with God's word written upon it. Then, he extends it in Trang's direction, signifying he was ready for combat.

"I said 'DRAW!'" Trang shouts, after seeing the scroll in Asoya's hand. By then, the rain has drenched the scroll, but Asoya continues to hold it in the direction of the one who was opposing him.

"This is my weapon of choice, I drew."

"Do you mock me with a scroll?"

"Red Velvet Shuriken, there is no mockery coming forth from me but newness. The words that are written upon this scroll are words that are sharper than any two edge ..."

While Asoya was talking, Trang takes out a dart and throws it at the scroll that was in Asoya's hand, pinning it against a tree. Asoya points, looks at his empty hand, then stares in the direction of his scroll, which was now pinned to a tree, and says, "Wow, I wasn't expecting that; that was my favorite scroll," as he points in the direction of the scroll that has Psalm 91 written on it.

As those words were still rolling off Asoya's tongue, Trang has already run upon him with his sword drawn out. Asoya barely notices Trang out of the corner of his eye but leans backward as Trang swings his sword upwards, scarcely missing Asoya's face.

Splash スプラッシュ! Water splashes everywhere as Asoya's back hits the ground. Asoya quickly pushes himself up off his back, performs a cartwheel with one hand, and then gets into his fighting position.

"Hrrmmmph, that was close, you nearly struck me."

Asoya's Sugegasa hat cracks with a line straight down the middle, then it falls off his head in two pieces; one piece fell on his left side and the other dropped on his right.

"Argghhh, that was my favorite hat! First my scroll now my hat?"

"Next, your life!"

Trang says as he scuttles up to Asoya swiftly and, without aim but with mere frustration, he swings his sword seven times. On the eighth swing, Trang brought his sword up, then drops it hard on Asoya. Seeing the force of Trang's blade, Asoya slightly opens his blade to catch Trang's attack. *CRASH* クラッシュ! Sparks fly upward as his sword meets Asoya's sword; the sparks soar to the ground, burning out once it touches the wet ground. Before Trang could draw back his sword to strike again, Asoya quickly closes Trang's sword into his sheath and sparks fly once again from their metal as Trang's blade slides across and scrapes against Asoya's.

Clink チャリンという音! Trang's blade was now pinned between Asoya's sheath and blade handle. He endeavors to yank it free, but Asoya's hold is firm. With one hand on his sheath and the other on the blade's handle, he turns his sword sideways then releases his hand from the handle, Asoya draws his fist back then digs it deep into Trang's chest, *POW!* Trang slides backwards while water splashes everywhere.

CHAPTER 11

SMOKE AND BAKUDAN'S 爆弾!

TO KEEP HIMSELF FROM FALLING, TRANG PLACES HIS
hand on the ground while he was sliding backwards due to the sheer
force of Asoya's blow, causing water to wallow between his fingers.
Once Trang gains his equanimity, he charges Asoya again with both
hands clutching his sword handle Trang oscillates his sword sideways and Asoya cartwheels with no hands over the blade, then did
a backflip with no hands, landing behind Trang. Asoya screams,
"Trang, no, please, stop this madness!"

"Stop? You want me to stop?! What did you expect to happen
when the clan's shadow is upon you? *We are clandestine*; this
shadow won't cease until it covers you. The only madness is your
betrayal."

敵意

Hostility

忠誠

"I don't wanna fight with you," insists Asoya.

Trang kicks Asoya in his stomach.

"Owww!" Asoya says from the sharp pain, both of his feet lift off of the ground while he skyrockets backwards. Trang takes out a star and catapults it at the one who deserted the clan. Asoya could not stop himself from being airborne; he sees the star coming in the midst of the heavy rainfall and places his sheathed blade in front of himself. The star makes contact with the sheath, ricocheting off of it. Asoya, still in the air from the power of Trang's kick, then crashes into a building and bursts through the wall. Now covered in debris, he lies there gripping his stomach. He wasn't just in pain, but his stomach has a throbbing sting coming from it. No one in or out of the clan has ever been able to hit him that hard, no one except the shadow known as the Red Velvet Shuriken.

He shakes the debris off himself and rises to his feet, slowly shaking his head and then holds the side of his head. Asoya was not able to recover from the assault before Trang struck again, three shining purple orbs bounce on the floor in the house he was in and lands a couple of inches from him.

"Bakudan's?" Asoya exclaims upon seeing the orbs, for he knew what they were, specially made bombs 爆弾. Smoke begins to proceed from them, and then they light up a light yellowish color.

"Let's see this *Kingdom Stuff* save you now." Trang says softly and mockingly with a sly grin on his face.

"He, he, he, heh, heh."

34

Asoya leaps into the other room of the house and crosses his arms over his head to brace himself for the explosion. Boom! KA-BOOM! 爆発 The three bombs went off, one right after the other. Asoya's scream echoes as the explosion overpowers the sound of his voice. Clouds of thick smoke cover the scene as large pieces of debris from the explosion fall in random places.

"This is what becomes of the ones who disobey our master."

CHAPTER 12

ACHING SCREAMS OF LOSS

TRANG TAKES OUT TWO THROWING STARS. DEBRIS from the explosion soars in his direction so he hurls the stars at the objects, stopping them from coming his way.

"Sheer mayhem," Trang says with his eyes closed, then opens them to see the debris continue to fall and smoke rising.

"Now, what did you say you were going to tell me about later? Some Kingdom stuff?" Trang asks as he frowns, squinting his eyes to see if he could find Asoya.

"Vermillion!" Trang shouts, calling for Asoya, but Asoya was lying down on top of a building, four buildings down while Trang searches for him, chanting out his name violently. Being silent while on a mission is second nature to an assassin; it's engraved in them, but in this instance, Trang tosses that philosophy aside. He continues to shout for Vermillion, his screams were as though he has just lost a limb or severed a finger; there was a certain pain and anger behind them. This anger was due to him losing a brother, someone he helped mold in the clan. Those who desert the clan are marked as dissidents 反抗. For ninjas, dissidence is simply not tolerated.

Asoya feels another sharp pain, but this pain was coming from his left arm. He reaches his right hand over gently to feel what it was, a small part of the building, some rubble has embedded itself in his arm from the explosion. He yanks it out as noiselessly as possible, and blood begins to flow down his arm. He reaches towards his left wrist and unravels the cloth that was wrapped around it, then he wraps his arm.

"Vermillion, you can't run from me forever…VERMILLION!"

"Trang …" Asoya said softly as he lay on top of the building, holding his sword in his arms, encasing in its sheath like a baby hiding himself from Trang.

"Red Velvet, my brother," Asoya says with pain in his voice as he hears the screams of his old friend calling his name. Trang stops searching and takes out a throwing star, spinning it in his hand; he then walks off. "Why him, Lord? Why him, why now? Not Trang," Asoya says as he gently climbs down the building he once took refuge in. The rain starts to subside. He remembers when he and Trang were at the head of their class during training on an obstacle course with thirty other young ninjas. Asoya was ten and Trang was twelve. They finish the obstacle course before any of the others did. Asoya came in first, Trang second.

"Asoya and Trang! Advance to the next obstacle." One of the instructors shouted, seeing that they made it in first. They bowed before their training instructor and rose up again.

Before they walked over to the next training site, Asoya walked over to where his sword was located; it was laying next to the ground under a tree. As he picked it up, Trang asked, "How is it that you are always one step ahead of me? I'm older than you; this should not be."

Asoya turned his head in Trang's direction and, with laughter in his voice, said, "Hey, you're the one who said that we are clandestine and taught me most of the stuff I know; don't look at me."

Trang looked up, realizing it to be true, he taught Asoya most of what he knew concerning battles and obstacles. Trang then said, "Clandestine? Oh yeah," as he scratched his own head. He then walked over to Asoya, placed his hand on his shoulder and said, "Well, you may have won this time, Asoya, but on this next obstacle course, I'm going to be ready for you, ha ha!" He winked his eye at Asoya.

As the memory begins to fade, Asoya looks down upon the wet ground and sees his reflection in a puddle of water. He frowns, then says, "Vermillion is not here; a Word Carrier has taken his place. My past no longer is."

Asoya then takes his scarf and brings it over his nose and mouth and takes part of his cloak covering his head to hide himself as he travels through the damp night.

CHAPTER 13

THE CLAN'S HIGH-RANKING FOUR

IN THE CLAN THAT ASOYA SEPARATED HIMSELF FROM—
four ninjas were ranked high above the rest. Asoya, who was ranked
first, was given the title *Ruthless Vermillion* by other ninjas within
his clan because of his callousness when taking out whoever their
master sent him after with no remorse 悔悟. Trang, who was ranked
second by choice when he could have been the first, was known as
the *Red Velvet Shuriken*. Gekijō, also known as *Shatter,* was ranked
third, and the fourth ninja was titled *Pendulum*. Pendulum was let
go from the clan, excommunicated 破門した for being too rebellious and not following the orders of their master.

Each of these four specialized in their own areas within the
clan, with traits making them valuable to their master. Asoya was
summoned for solo missions ソロミッション that were high pri-
ority and considered impossible; what would normally take a team
of ten ninjas to do, Asoya would do by himself. When it came to

hand-to-hand combat, no one was more brutal or precise than he. Trang specialized in undercover assignments; secret covert operation 秘密の割り当て and battlefield strategies. He was titled the Red Velvet Shuriken for the number of victims he took out with his specially made throwing stars; Trang did not miss his targets. He is strategic on the field of battle. No one was more accurate when hitting a target with weaponry.

Gekijō was an expert in finding deserters from the clan, a tracker トラッカー. He would always find those who tried to run or escape from their master. He also had an obsession with making things explode, causing panic and disarray. The fourth ninja was proficient in setting impossible to detect traps トラップ and entangling his victims in ropes; he would watch them dangle, swinging back and forth like a pendulum; thus, he earned the name Pendulum. He would have been ranked third, but his hard-headedness, his disrespect and his rebellious nature caused him to be lowered a rank, putting Shatter above him. Shatter, too, was wild but always fell in line and followed their master's wishes without hesitation.

Trang, the Red Velvet Shuriken, who cleaves to the ways of the shadow and the law along with the oaths of the clan, is now on the hunt for Asoya, the light, for Asoya has now become a candle.

CHAPTER 14

THE ABANDONED GOVERNOR'S BUILDING

TRANG TRAVELS SPRINTING THROUGH THE SHADOWS, and when he needs more cover, he jumps into the trees. He stops running and pulls out a map. The moon's light illuminates the paper, allowing him to see where his location was on the document. This lead Trang to the location where Asoya and Shatter had their battle, the abandoned governor's building. He folds the document, places it back within his shirt, and continues running using the shadows for concealment.

He makes it to the abandoned building and takes out a climbing device called the *Kaginawa* 鈎縄. The Kaginawa is an iron hook tied to a rope; the hook grips whatever it is thrown on. He twirls the rope around several times before releasing it upwards. It almost makes it to the top of the building; the iron hook latches onto one of the tiles and wedges itself in. Trang tugs on it, making sure it could hold his body weight. He begins the climb up. Once inside on the top floor, he lowers the black cloth that covers his nose and mouth.

"Gekijō was the tracker amongst us, his efforts to capture Vermillion has been reduced to ashes," he says looking around at the rubble where he sees that multiple explosives went off, causing the top floor to be unstable. He takes out a document and read what it said about Shatter, that he could no longer speak or use his right arm from the injury he sustained when he fell through the floor.

CHAPTER 15

TRANG'S LAST MEMORY OF ASOYA AND SHATTER

AS TRANG EXAMINES THE ROOM, HE THINKS ABOUT the last time he saw Shatter and Asoya in the clan. Trang watched Asoya train as he sat in the doorway, polishing his throwing stars. Asoya was blindfolded; striking a wooden post, that was in the shape of a person while avoiding throwing stars that flew his way from various ninjas. These ninjas were in four separate corners of the room. As he watched Asoya, the ninja named Gekijō, also known as Shatter, tried to sneak up behind him, but he was aware of Shatter's presence.

"Move again in my direction, and you will see for yourself why they call me the Shuriken."

"How did you know that I was near?" Shatter asked, puzzled as he removed his metal mask from around his face.

"Your scent … you reek of explosive powder and stale smoke," Trang said, lifting one of his polished stars and seeing Shatter's reflection in it. Shatter moved from behind Trang and stood beside him but a distance off. Shatter folded his arms as he watched Asoya hit the training dummy, chipping away at the wood with his fists while avoiding being hit by throwing stars that were being hurled randomly.

"There is not a ninja in this clan that is made like this one," Shatter said, seeing Asoya escape two stars and then break the arm off the wooden dummy with a single kick.

"What would you do if Vermillion abandoned the clan?"

"Abandoned? You speak folly Gekijō; there is none who is more devoted to missions than him," Trang said, looking over at Shatter, where he saw Shatter frowning as he watched Asoya train and studied his movements. Trang looked back at Asoya, then answered his question.

"Dissidence is not tolerated from any assassin in this clan, not even Ruthless … now, stop talking," Trang said as he continued polishing his stars. Shatter grinned, chuckling softly.

"I'm not being factious, but seriously, if Vermillion fled and you caught up with him, and he drew out his sword against yours, what would you do? Would you fight him?"

"Enough," Trang said as he stopped polishing momentarily, staring down at his star, not blinking.

"Vermillion versus Red Velvet, come one, come all and see this play. This battle will be epic. Come and witness the soiree ... metal versus metal, and steel versus steel—who will be left standing between the two, only time will reveal."

Trang dropped the star as well as the cloth that was in his hands forcefully as he rose off the floor.

"Your bantering ceases now."

"So, you wanna play?" Shatter asked as he took out a bomb and started to light the fuse on it. He then looked at Trang and said, "Let us have an on-stage performance worthy of being watched."

Without hesitation, Trang sent a cascade of razor-sharp spinners in Shatter's direction.

"Are you CRAZY?" Shatter asked as he tried everything within his power to avoid the fastidiousness of Trang's throwing stars. It almost looked as if Shatter was doing ballet, but not intentionally.

"Crazy? That answer is simple —YES!" Trang replied as he ran over to Shatter and socked him on the arm, then dug his elbow in his side that he held the bomb with ひじを掘る. Shatter's arm muscles weakened as he dropped the bomb. Before it hit the ground, Trang grabbed it and pulled the fuse out. He then lifted Shatter into the air using one arm and slammed his back against the wall.

46

CHAPTER 16

KEIKOKU, WARNING 警告

SHATTER'S FEET DANGLED AS HE TRIED TO WEASEL himself free from Trang's hold.

"You play far too many games to be a member of this clan. Assassins don't play; they kill 殺す. Speak against the assassin that has the highest honors among us again, and not even master will be able to find your body," Trang said, taking out another star and pointing it at Shatter with his free hand. He lifted Shatter just a tad bit higher and scraped his throwing star against Shatter's metal mask. It made a screeching-like sound.

"Vermillion, help me, HELP ME! Red Velvet is picking on me! Boo-hoo, BOO-HOOO!" Shatter shouted in a whimpering baby-like voice.

Asoya ran out of the training room and unsheathed his blade. "Red Velvet, put Shatter down."

Trang's eyes were fixed on Shatter's, so they didn't blink once. Seeing Trang's unwavering resolve, Asoya reminded him of what their master told them.

"Master said that we are NOT allowed to fight against one another; he said that we are family. Though we three are the highest ranking in this clan, we, like the other foot-solider ninja, must abide by the words of Master. This is the law of those who dwell in clans, and the law amongst assassins."

Trang finally blinked; he turned his head and looked at Asoya, whose face was serious and very devoted to the words he just spoke. *The law…*Trang thought as he looked down at the scars that covered Asoya's body, then nodded his head in agreement. He dropped Shatter, who then hit the floor, sat up, and removed his metal mask, laughing historically.

"Enough, Shatter!" Asoya said, pointing the sharp end of his blade at Shatter. "Master told you to stop picking, frolicking and jesting with the other ninja, especially those amid the ranks."

Shatter stretched out his bottom lip as it started to quiver; he had a sad look on his face as though he were about to cry.

"You're not gonna tell on me, are you, tattletale, tale toddle waddle?" Shatter said mockingly, in a baby's voice. Asoya walked over to Shatter and touched his sword on Shatter's shoulder. Shatter looked at it and responded with cheer.

"You're going to dove me with your sword just as the kings do in other nations when giving a knight their power. This is so

48

EXCITING, handing me your position as the highest-ranking one, you're so thoughtful."

"Gekijō, do not become master's enemy by not listening to what he told you. If you do, you will, in turn, become my enemy. I'm tired of issuing *keikokus* to you; this is your last warning."

Keikoku's comments, by definition, are warnings 警告. Shatter got off his knees and sat with his back against the wall; he lifted his metal mask over his face.

"You two are so tedious … and annoying, no respect for humor," Shatter said, frowning.

Asoya turned to looked at Trang, frowning at him; Asoya sheathed his sword without breaking his gaze. After staring at Trang for some time, he walked back into the training room and continued to train.

"Did you see the way Vermillion looked at you? So ruthlessly …" Shatter said with laughter in his voice.

"Vermillion versus Red Velvet. Now *that* would be a cotillion," he said taking out a bomb and looking up at Trang who turned and headed back over to the door to continue to watch Asoya train as he finished polishing his throwing stars.

The present:

Trang stops thinking about his last memory of Shatter and Asoya and starts to laugh quietly at first. After a minute or so, his laughter got louder; it was almost as though he were drunk.

"Who knew that the words that you spoke that day would become a reality? Gekijō…" he says kneeling down and picking up one of Shatter's bombs off the floor. He rubs the soot off to see the words written on the bomb: 'Kush'. He sets it back on the floor and rises slowly.

"Everything Shatter and the spy told me was true. Vermilion has strayed from us. He has committed dissidence."

He glances out of the window and sees the moon.

"You should not have done this, brother," he says, placing his hand over his face with sadness. He slowly lowers his hand from his face as his core starts to take over, the core of the clan. He balls up his fists and frowns, turning away from the window and walking to the middle of the room.

"Separation from us is a mistake that you shall regret dearly."

Trang pulls his hood over his head then places his mask over his nose and mouth.

"You have faced many shadows, but NEVER have you faced a shadow like me!" he shouts as he runs and jumps out of the top story window, soaring down towards the trees.

CHAPTER 17

THE VALERIAN ROOT

TWO DAYS HAVE PASSED, AND IT IS NIGHT. ASOYA SEES that the dark green leaves hanging upon the trees are starting to fade slightly.

"The leaves have started to change; autumn 秋 is approaching," he says, looking at a leaf that sways from being pushed upon by the evening wind. He then looks up at the sky.

Like a boat that drifts delicately off the shore and into the sea, so do the night clouds float, crossing the stars and bright light of the moon. Asoya drinks some water from a nearby spring. When he has had his fill, he goes to the inn that he was staying at a few days prior and sets his cased sword by the door. He slides the door shut behind himself and then lights a candle, setting it down upon a small wooden table, he finally gets to rest from his travels.

He sits down, takes out his dagger and assesses it; it has not lost its sharpness, so he cleans it, then spins it around one hand and puts it down on the table. Asoya tends to his injuries by grinding up a root known as *Valerian* バレリアンルート, which comes from a class of perennial plants. The past two days, he has just used fresh bandages and water; now, he has the root. Like a flower, this plant is the perfect remedy for *joint and muscle pain*. He cleans the wound on his arm that he patched up two days prior from the debris and then patches it up again using a fresh cloth and bandage. When done, he rubs the valerian root on his muscles and joints, allowing it to set in.

He usually only had to use such remedies when going up against fifty or more ninjas at a time in enemy territory or after a training session that lasted for hours when he was in the clan. Still, crossing paths with a hitman like Trang causes him to need such remedies again. Trang—one man, one ninja, one hitman. This leaves Asoya somewhat confounded.

"Shadows ..." he says to himself, for a shadow from his past has sprung up; a past shadow from the clan has made himself known. He feels lost and needs direction, so he decides to do what the Word Carrier before him did, go to the Creator of all things, the Lord God, the Almighty One.

CHAPTER 18

DWELLING IN THE SECRET PLACE

ASOYA HUMBLES HIMSELF BY GETTING ON HIS KNEES. With eyes closed, he lifts both of his hands towards the ceiling. A surrender 降伏 position, his palms face upwards as he spoke to The Creator of all things.

"My Lord and Master, you are the Omnipotent One. All power belongs to you; it is in your hands. All flesh must come to you, even those who reside in the land of Japan. It is written in your Word that he that dwelleth in the secret place of the Most High shall abide under the shadow of the Almighty. As it says in Psalm 91:1 and Matthew 6:6, Master, you are The Almighty, the Most High."

He lowers one of his hands and says, placing his hand over his heart, "I will say of the LORD, You are my refuge and my fortress, my God; in You will I trust."

Lowering his hands and looking back at his sheathed blade, he then looks up at the ceiling, closes his eyes, and raises his hands, saying,

"In you will I trust Master and not my blade nor the clan as I was once taught."

As one of the scrolls starts to glow and flicker, he opens his eyes, seeing it glow, unravels it, and when he does, words rise off the page. Glowing gold, the words come from Psalms 46:10, which read, "Be still, and know that I am God: I will be exalted among the heathen (those who do not know or serve me), I will be exalted in the earth."

"Yes, Master ..." says Asoya upon reading the words and receiving his instructions. Asoya lifts his hands once again as a form of surrender and reverence to the Lord, the Most High, and says, "I will exalt you among those who do not know you. I will elevate and lift you high upon the earth."

The words that he sees glowing before his face start to encircle his body then enter his heart. Each time it enters, his chest glows brighter. He grabs his chest as he falls to the floor, catching himself with his other hand. His eyes glow gold and then turn back to normal.

"Whenever I spend personal time with you and in your Word, I am dwelling in your secret place, that personal place that is between you and me. I dwell in your secret place, Master, for you are The Almighty. I desire to abide under your shadow," Asoya speaks as he kneels low to the floor, giving praise to the God of Heaven. His chest flashes red; he was warned that danger was approaching.

"Thank you, Master," He says as he gets up off the floor. Subtly reaching for his dagger, he grips it with readiness. "A past shadow from my old clan is on the chase." he says, understanding that it was a ninja he was just warned about, a shadow from his past. A golden throwing star smashes through the window, Asoya ducks and rolls on the wood floor as it passes him like a bat. The star thwacks into the wall, embedding itself deep within the wall, causing the star to vibrate from the impact. Asoya glances back at the wall seeing the star.

CHAPTER 19

THE TUSSLING

"A GOLDEN SHURIKEN ...TRANG..."

He says, knowing who the star belongs to. More stars follow, and no matter where Asoya moves, they chase after him. Each star was aimed at a vital part of his body. Asoya refracts them, but not without strain or effort for his hand starts to hurt from deflecting the sharp projectiles. Trang threw them with such lethal force that it was difficult for Asoya to keep his dagger in his hand. Eventually, the stars stop coming, and there was silence.

Asoya was still, and his dagger faces the window, but Trang came in another way; he crashes through the front door, rolls on the floor, and then throws two more stars. One scrapes Asoya's wrist and the other his ankle. Asoya simply was not fast enough to avoid the precision of this ninja. Trang rises off the ground slowly, and says,

"Gekijō failed to bring you in for your disloyalty; now I'm after you."

Asoya lifts his dagger slowly in Trang's direction, not wanting to fight but knowing that there was no escape from Trang.

"Dissidence is not tolerated," Trang says as he takes out two more gold-plated stars. The veins in Trang's arms pulsate as the muscles in his arms tighten from him gripping his throwing stars with potency.

"Beware my shurikens."

Collision

Asoya takes a deep breath preparing for a barrage of shurikens to fly his way, for Asoya is leery of no one in the clan, save this one, Red Velvet. Once Red Velvet has a target in his sights, his stars do not stop until they make contact. As a golden star twirls at Asoya, Asoya catapults his arm as though it were a battering ram, deflecting the star with his dagger. A second star follows the first; this time, Asoya swings his arm so hard that he almost loses his balance.

His dagger chips from Trang throwing it so hard. It was the third star that Asoya was not prepared for, for it makes contact with Asoya's shoulder. Asoya drops his dagger, grabbing his arm in pain. Trang struck a nerve in his arm, causing his arm to go limp and numb.

CHAPTER 20

THE VULNERABILITY

ASOYA DOES NOT REMOVE THE STAR, KNOWING THAT it was deeply embedded, but he does hit a pressure point on his arm, which allows him to have temporary function of it. Now that he has feeling in his arm, Asoya takes out a smoke bomb and breaks it on the wood floor. It explodes as smoke consumes the room, which is perfect cover for Asoya, so he issues a 奇襲攻撃 sneak attack. He throws a flash bomb at Trang's face. Trang, thinking it was merely a stone casts a star at it; the star makes contact with the bomb as it flashes light in Trang's eyes, temporarily blinding him, Asoya uses this time to his advantage. He sneaks up behind Trang to strike him on the area between his shoulder and neck but Trang is aware of his presence; even without his sight, he senses Asoya and catches Asoya's fist.

"A ninja sees with more than just their eyes. To think otherwise is a blunder. You have been away from the clan for far too long for you have forgotten that it was I who has taught you that sneak attack," Trang says as his sight starts to return. With his other hand, Asoya quickly attempts to bury his fist in Trang's lower back, but Trang catches his fist with his other hand and grips it with tightness; now both of Asoya's hands are bound by Trang's. He tries to free both of his hands from Trang's grip but cannot pry them loose.

"There is a vulnerability in your last two attacks, here, allow me to show it to you," Trang says as he releases both of Asoya's hands and quickly turns low to the ground striking Asoya on his hip, *SNAP* スナップ! Trang knocks Asoya's hipbone 股関節の骨 out of its socket. As Asoya tumbles over due to not being able to put pressure on his dislocated hip, Trang struck him on the stomach two times, then lifts Asoya high into the air using both arms. After a moment of staring at Asoya's face, Trang slams him hard on the floor back first. The floor cracks as the air is knocked out of Asoya's lungs a second time. Trang looks down at Asoya as he sees him struggling to breathe. Asoya's discomfort was excruciating, for there was no mercy in that attack. No remorse. With disdain, he watches Asoya suffer, trying wheeze and gasp for air. Once Trang finishes gawking, he speaks, "This is the flaw in your attack; it leaves your legs wide open."

CHAPTER 21

THE GLOWING GOLDEN WORDS

ASOYA FINALLY CATCHES HIS BREATH, AND AS HE DOES, the pressure point that Asoya struck allowing him to have temporary use of his injured arm wears off. He pops his hip back in its socket, sits up on his knees, and holds his arm close to the shoulder area. Asoya laughs but blithely, Trang notices and says,

"You are laughing, do tell what you think is so funny,"

Asoya sighs and explains as he rubs his stomach.

"If you really must know, I will tell you. Earlier this evening, I ate three curry buns with extra beans in them, and ever since I ate them, I have had gas stuck right here in my abdomen area. When you struck me twice in the stomach, I burped twice in your face, and you didn't even notice. Ah, now I feel a great deal of relief; the gas is gone, and it is all thanks to you."

Trang was prepared to throw another star but stops. His arm was in the air, and his star faces the ceiling when he sees Asoya holding his arm. He knows that the star was wedged deeply in Asoya's arm. He lowers his shuriken, and looks at it, frowning. He pulls down the cloth that covers his nose and mouth.

"You know the law," Trang says as he spins the star in his hand, the star glistens. He glances at Asoya, points the shuriken at him, and continues to speak. "You know that those who are pledged to the shadows do not leave them. There are rules; you comprehend this. There are no truces for the ones who scurry away and run from the clan, not even for Vermillion, the highest-ranking amongst us."

Asoya looks over at one of the scrolls on the table that contains God's word and then back at Trang as he applies pressure on his own arm to push back some of the pain. The core and philosophy of what it means to be a ninja takes over Trang.

"I told you to beware," he says with a grin as he pinches his gold-plated stars and tosses two at Asoya. The stars hit an invisible barrier, some sort of wall that natural weapons could not get past.

"What's this?" Trang asks. As he sees his stars repel in separate directions away from Asoya, he grabs two more shurikens and tosses them harder than the first two. Asoya's eyes glow gold around the iris area as God's word proceeds from his chest and shields him. One star is knocked away from his body, than a second. Trang then sees gold glowing words start to be visible, surrounding Asoya. The words from Psalm 91:1 read, "The shadow of The Almighty."

"The shadow of The Almighty? What is this shadow?" Trang asks, backing up a few feet pointing his throwing stars at the words.

CHAPTER 22

CLANDESTINE 秘密

BREATHING HEAVILY, ASOYA QUICKLY ROLLS ACROSS the floor and does a one-handed backflip as he grabs his sheath blade that was propped up against the wall. His eyes stop glowing as the golden words start to become invisible and disappear from Trang's sight.

"Yes, that's it," Trang says with resolve. "Extract your blade and raise it against me just like Gekijō said that you would. Give me a reason to volley you with my shurikens." Trang takes out four more throwing stars.

"No!" Asoya shouts, looking at his sword hand then back at Trang.

"As it says in Psalm 91:2, 'The Lord is my refuge and my fortress: my God; in HIM will I trust.' He is my trust and NOT my blade!" Asoya shouts, taking out two firecrackers 火のクラッカー and catapults them at Trang. The firecrackers were disguised as rocks, and Trang, believing them to be rocks, hits both of them with his throwing stars. When they make contact with the firecrackers, they erupt, making loud popping sounds, bursts of glowing sparkles and fizzing noises, and because of this, there was a faint haze separating Asoya and Trang.

As Trang is distracted by the commotion, Asoya took off his brown cloak and tosses it at Trang, who unsheathes his sword and cuts the cloak right down the middle, expecting Asoya to be right behind it. However, Trang is met with another flare, which smashes against his chest and creates a bright, luminous, blinding light. Asoya then kicks Trang in the chest, sending him flying through the wall, and Asoya uses this time to escape by crashing through one of the windows.

Trang lays there covered by wood and paper, not because he was hurt but in disbelief because of Asoya's dissidence from the clan. He simply can't understand what would make Asoya leave their ways. His sight starts to be restored, and after some time passes, he gets up slowly, staring at his gold-plated shuriken. He walks over to the window that Asoya jumped out of and says, "You are different somehow; your moves and attacks are non-lethal, and apart from that, your use of weaponry and covertness, I see you have not forgotten what I have taught you."

He does not pursue Asoya but goes the opposite direction, dashing through the trees.

"I have not forgotten what you have taught me, Trang, we are clandestine," Asoya says quietly with sadness while hiding behind a tree and looking down at his sword. "Clandestine 秘密," he says a second time; he then travels using the night shadows to remain unseen.

CHAPTER 23

ASOYA AND THE KAMPO PHYSICIAN 内科医

ASOYA KNOWS A PHYSICIAN THAT LIVES IN A VILLAGE

about an hour's journey away. The physician's name is *Kazuki,* a Kampo 漢方医学 physician who specializes in natural plants and herbs for healing. He was also very skilled in the human anatomy 人体解剖学. When it comes to any type of injury that is past sickness, Asoya travels to him. He arrives at physician's home late in the evening. He knocks on the door, and after a moment, Kazuki opens the door, but just a crack because he did not know who it was.

"Peace be unto you and your home, physician Kazuki, it is I," says Asoya.

"The Word Carrier," Kazuki says, opening his door just a little wider, being at peace now. Asoya sees the physician's wife and daughter asleep on their mats.

"Pardon my intrusion at this hour; I would not have come if it were not urgent."

The physician sees Asoya holding his arm with his scarf.

"No need for pardons. I appreciate all that you have done for my family and me. If it were not for your donations, I would not be able to afford the imports of the herbs and plants that come from outside Japan. I will meet you around back."

Asoya bows his head to give thanks, and Kazuki gently closes the door. There is a house directly behind the physician's home that is used for his clinic and study. Before walking to the back, Asoya looks around cautiously and hides his weapons under a bush. At the clinic, the physician lights four lanterns and three candles. Asoya sits down.

"Isn't Kampo the Chinese practice of medicine? What made you take it up?" Asoya asks as he looks around at all the Chinese writings on the wall next to drawings of various plants.

"Are not the words that you are carrying from the Hebrew people?" Kazuki replies as he points at one of Asoya's scrolls.

Asoya chuckles. "These words that I carry have indeed come from the Hebrew people, but they are for ALL people, for the words contained within these scrolls came from the very mouth of God, the God of all flesh, that includes the Japanese people."

Kazuki smiles.

"Medicine is medicine, whether from China, Africa, or India, and any good physician will take up any practice that is beneficial for the health and well-being of the people. The physicians from the land of China have an intricate understanding of natural medicine, from herbs to plants that come from the earth, so I decided to become a student."

"Fair enough, a physician is a physician no matter where they have learned their profession. Kazuki, I come to you because you are the best at what you do." says Asoya.

"Let's see what we are working with."

Asoya removes his scarf from his shoulder.

"Some sort of projectile has lodged itself deep into your arm. It has torn through your deltoid muscle and is stuck amid your humerus and greater tubercle bone. This is usually a fatal injury," Kazuki says as he rises to picks up one of the candles. "How did this happen, Word Carrier?"

Asoya spoke nothing, only stares at the lanterns. The physician walks back over to Asoya, shining the candle on his arm close to his shoulder. After further examining his arm, the physician backs up, shaking with fear and almost tripping over his own feet.

"That … that is a shuriken."

CHAPTER 24

KAZUKI'S DECISION

"IT IS AS YOU HAVE SPOKEN. I WOULD HAVE REMOVED it myself, but I know it had reached the bone and is stuck, so only a specialist can remove it, and you are that person, Kazuki."

He looks at the star on Asoya's arm, then responds.

"I knew there was something different about you. I just couldn't put my finger on what it was. How cautious you are. This attack was precise and not accidental; no one sustains such injuries and lives to tell unless they were once one of them."

Asoya stops looking down at his arm and looks up at Kazuki who continues speaking.

"Only a ninja can escape a ninja. I want no part of this, the whispers, the shadows. I sincerely appreciate what you have done for me and my family, but I don't want any trouble with clans, with shadows … with ninja."

"I am not a ninja, not anymore. I am a carrier of God's word now. Kazuki, no one can do what you do. You are the only one I know of who can properly treat and address this type of wound. After you assist me on this matter, I shall not return to this home."

The doctor thinks for a second, and after pacing the floor for over a minute, he sighs.

"I apologize for speaking to you out of fear. My job is to aid and assist anyone that needs it. I can tell by your actions that you are no longer a ninja. Alright, Word Carrier, I shall help you."

The doctor washes and prepares his tools to both remove and clean Asoya's wound. His back is turned as he prepares his tools. Asoya sighs as he looks at his injured shoulder, knowing why the shuriken was in it; it was there because of his disloyalty to the clan and rebellion from the shadows. Discouragement starts to set in. The scroll he was holding in his hand begins to glow. He looks down at it and pauses before opening it up. Words from the book of Jeremiah chapter thirty-two and verse twenty-seven start to rise off the page, glowing gold and appear before his face. "Behold, I am the LORD, the God of all flesh: is there anything too hard for me?"

After reading those words, Asoya replies, "No, Almighty One, there is nothing too hard for you."

The scroll stops glowing, and the gold words turn invisible. His chest glows and flashes red, and suddenly the words (Psalm 46:10)—that he was meditating on before Trang attacked him—proceed from his heart and flash gold before his face: "Be still and know that I am God: I will be exalted (raised and lifted high) among the heathen (those who do not trust in or follow me), I will be exalted in the earth."

Upon reading those words, Asoya speaks softly. "Yes, Master, you will be exalted and lifted high. I will exalt you among the people; I will exalt you amongst those who do not know you on this earth."

"Did you say something?" the physician asks as he turns and faces Asoya.

"I did. Have you heard about the shadow of The Almighty?"

The Physician hesitates to answer, thinking his words have something to do with ninja.

"This is a different type of shadow, not one that comes from the earth, nor from ninja but from above. Those who dwell in God and spend personal time with Him shall abide under His shadow."

The Physician relaxes and grabs his tools as he listens to Asoya's words. He starts to take the shuriken from his shoulder. As he does, Asoya doesn't even flinch but continues to speak about the shadow of The Almighty. The physician patches up the wound, putting warm ointment on it to numb the pain. He sews it up, then puts a substance around and on the wound that looks like mud; it is natural herbs with healing properties.

CHAPTER 25

THE TWO WOODEN BUCKETS

ASOYA WOULD OFFER HELP TO PEOPLE THAT WERE IN his surrounding communities free of charge, whether it was getting groceries for them or helping them build, repair, or rake leaves. With his extra time apart from doing Matthew 6:6 and praying in private, he helps others. There is one particular lady, Chiasa, whom he would help quite often, as she was in her late seventies and would soon be eighty. She volunteers twice a week at the orphanage that Elisa runs.

Chiasa enjoys teaching the children; it is one of the highlights of her week. She's teaches the children how to write traditional Japanese *kanji* characters 伝統的な漢字. On this particular day, Asoya was helping repair one of her wooden tables. As he repairs it, he teaches by referring to Psalm 91:4, "He (The Almighty, The Omnipotent One) shall cover thee with his feathers, and under his wings shalt thou trust: his truth shall be thy shield and buckler."

Continuing on, he says, "The Almighty himself shall cover you, and under His covering, His very protection shall you trust."

Chiasa paints Japanese kanji letters as she listens to Asoya. She dips her brush in black ink and rubs the brush across the page.

"His truths, the truths that come from His word shall be your shield," he says as he turns the table over. He makes sure that the legs on it are even. He measures it by using a bowl half-filled with water. Making sure the water doesn't shift to one side more than the other. If it was uneven, the table will not yet be fixed, and one leg on the table will be longer than the other.

"The truths of His word are a *buckler* バックラー, which is a shield that surrounds you on every side."

"On every side?" she asks as she ceases her brush-strokes and looks over at Asoya.

"Yes, on every side," he says with a smile, and seeing that the table was now level, he removes the bowl.

"If you need anything else fixed, just let me know. I am going to get you some water from one of the wells from a farmer who lives close by."

Asoya leaves and makes the trip to the farmer's well after filling two of Chiasa's buckets with water. He then makes the thirty-eight-minute walk back to her home. He carries two wood buckets connected by a thick wood stick over his shoulders. As he walks, though the buckets were filled to the top, none of the water spills out. Chiasa is going to use one bucket of water for cooking a stew, and the other will be used for cleaning. As he walks, a gold-plated star smashes into the stick that held the buckets together, causing the two buckets to crash to the ground, spilling the water.

"One hit!" a voice said from one of the nearby trees.

"Trang!" Asoya exclaims as he quickly reaches for his dagger. A second golden star spins and clashes against the dagger, knocking it from Asoya's hand.

"Two hits!" Trang said as Asoya's dagger twirls wildly in the air and then hits the ground. Asoya grabs his sword with haste from around his back, but before he could unsheathe it, a third star soars his way, hitting his sheathed weapon; it too was knocked from Asoya's grasp.

"Three hits."

Asoya looks down at his dagger and his sword that are lying on the ground. He knew that if he attempted to make a move, Trang would strike, so he stood still, only moving his eyes trying to search for Trang's position.

"There is only one hit left, and that is the man. He he he hah ha haa HITMAN! Now I see why Gekijō played so much; it lightens the mood and provides some entertainment. What do you think, Vermillion?" says Trang.

"I am NOT Vermillion! My name is Asoya; Asoya, the Word Carrier!" Asoya shouts in frustration at hearing his shadow name. He continues looking around, waiting for the last star to be thrown,

but no star came; there was only quietness as the wind blows a few leaves past Asoya.

End of *Asoya*: **Shadows From the Past**:
Trang (忍者、ヒットマン) Section 1

ワードキャリア
The Word Carrier

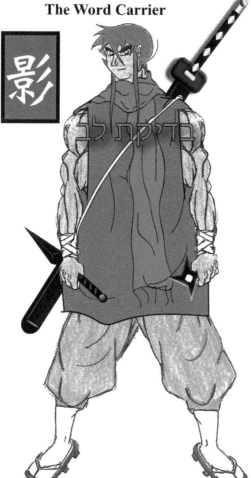

静止
Stillness

Be still, and know (*understand*) that I am God: I will be exalted among the heathen, (*the unbelievers, those who do not worship me*) I will be exalted in the earth.

(Psalms 46:10)

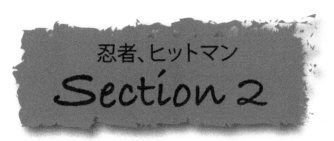

The Light, the Shuriken, and the Shadow

光　　　手裏剣　　　影

CHAPTER 26

THE ART OF ATTRITION

ON THE BATTLEFIELD, MANY DIFFERENT STRATEGIES
and tactics are used to take out an opponent. Some use the rush approach: go in, get the job done, then flee the scene. Others use the bombardment method, continually sticking your opponent with a certain string of attacks at once until it overwhelms them, causing them to either surrender or be defeated. Then, there are those who use the slow approach that is steady and gradual. This methodology has a purpose, to ease in, tearing away at a person's defenses and their strengths using sustained attacks to knock them off-kilter, moving them off balance so much that their internal harmony has been disturbed. In a sense, it causes mental fatigue. This methodology is known as the art of attrition 消耗戦. It is this style and method that the assassin called the Red Velvet Shuriken, also known as Trang, prefers to use.

CHAPTER 27

FEAR 恐れ

TRANG'S LAST ATTACK LEFT ASOYA SOMEWHAT SHAKEN, and fear started to set in. Fear was something that was foreign to Asoya, for he fears no one that walks in the flesh. He only fears The Almighty and the guardians, but not man. Trang was no ordinary man; however, he was a hitman, a Koroshiya, a ninja ranked second but only by choice in the clan. In Asoya's eyes, Trang was the true highest-ranking assassin.

When it came to this sudden fear, it was not the fear of the hitman himself, but rather the fear of the unknown: what might happen due to Trang being a field and combat strategist. Though he starts to feel fear, the Lord speaks to him through his heart what is written in Psalms 46:10: "Be still (calm, quiet), and know that I am God: I will be exalted among the heathen (those who do now know, serve or worship me), I will be exalted in the earth."

After hearing these words within himself, Asoya unravels the scroll containing Psalm 91; he reads verses five and six out loud: "Thou shalt not be afraid for the terror (extreme fear caused by violence) by night; nor for the arrow (darts or weapons) that flieth by day; Nor for the pestilence that walketh in darkness; nor for the destruction that wasteth at noonday."

"No matter what, I shall not be afraid," he says, looking up from the scroll, which he then rolls up, and after doing a few pushups, he heads out the door to exalt the Lord and make Him known among the people.

CHAPTER 28

ELISA HANAKOTOBA

RAINY DAYS ARE ABUNDANT DURING THIS TIME IN Japan; some days, the showers are light, and on others, it falls with heaviness. Because of the multiple rainy days, a flower begins to grow and bloom that is called the *Ajisai*.

Elisa was taking care of a group of children and was out for a walk with them when she tells them to stop walking for a moment. She smiles as she reaches down and picks a couple of the Ajisai flowers, placing them in her woven basket. All of the children watch her and smile. Elisa Hanakotoba, a young woman of Japanese and Spanish descent, is in her early twenties who sees beauty in every season.

Her father was an entrepreneur who believed that there was beauty in all cultures, no matter the nationality or the land a person was from. Her mother was from Spain and was a traditional Spanish dancer. Elisa's mother was fluent in the dances of

Fandango, *Muineira* and *Flamenco*. She was also a singer. Elisa's father fell in love with the dancer/singer the moment he laid eyes on her. She was buying spices at a nearby market when he had traveled to Spain for a business deal. He went against tradition and married her; they had one child, a lovely daughter, Elisa. On one rainy day, tragedy befell her parents, causing her to be an orphan. After many days of being alone without food or someone to care for her, Chiasa found Elisa crying and hiding in a basket. She cried not from hunger but because she missed her father and her mother.

Chiasa took her into her home and raised Elisa as though she were her own child, teaching her many things, one of which was how to filter her pain from her loss and guide it through the art that she creates, the art of self-expression. Art is Elisa's passion, but she also has a second passion, and that passion is helping and raising children. As a result of Elisa's understanding of what it was like to be without family that is blood-related, she opened an orphanage with the money that her father left behind.

秋
Autumn

I love when the season of Aki is near, (Autumn) It is my favorite because of this flower, a flower that's called *Ajisai* which blooms from the heavy rainfall.

あじさい
Ajisai

Elisa Hanakotoba

CHAPTER 29

THE KOROSHIYA AND THE GUARDIAN 守護天使

ASOYA TRAVELS TO AN ORPHANAGE THAT HE HAS BEEN to on many occasions to speak to the children. It has been a month since he has been there, and he knows that they desire to hear him tell his stories, so he makes a trip there. When he arrives, all the children surround him excitedly and are happy to see him. He pats a few of them on the head, and he sees Hanakotoba, but no one calls her by that name; they only call her Elisa. He asks her if it is okay for him to tell the children a story, Elisa smiles and nods yes. He sits down on a woven mat and places his sheathed sword in front of himself gently. All the children sit down, waiting to hear more stories. The other workers were ardent to hear him speak as well.

Elisa walks to the back of the room and sits down. She begins to paint *Kaneshon* and Ajisai flowers because the Ajisai flower thrives during the rainy seasons, the season of Tsuyu 梅雨, and

87

has become one of her favorites. She smiles, but this smile was not from painting but due to Asoya taking time out of his busy travel schedule to speak with the children.

"There was a man who was a Koroshiya," Asoya says after taking a deep breath and looking down at his sword. As he reaches down and touches it, he removes his hand and looks up, watching the children; they are quiet, listening.

Koroshiya? Elisa thinks, and then stops painting and looks over at Asoya with concern. Her concern was not a result of what he might tell the children but over him speaking about past things that might cause him unneeded and unnecessary pain. He knows that she is looking at him; he looks over at her and smiles and, in so doing, lets her know with his face that everything was going to be okay. She nods, and with a faint smile, continues to paint.

"Hey…" Gēto says, "Tell us more about this man who was a Koroshiya, please."

Asoya chuckles as he continues the story. "The Koroshiya was not nice at all; he was cold-hearted, callus; he was a ninja."

"A ninja?" Gēto asks with excitement and surprise. "Are you a ninja, Masutā Asoya?"

"I am a Word Carrier. And Masutā? I am not your Master; stop calling me Master, boy," Asoya says with sternness as he frowns at Gēto. At the orphanage, Gēto was known for getting into mischief, so for Asoya to rebuke him so openly in front of everyone made the children laugh so loudly that even the workers snickered.

"Someone's in trouble," one of the small children said as they point and laugh at Gēto.

Elisa stands up, "Settle down, children, settle down." she says calmly but loud enough for all the little ones to hear, "Let Mr. Asoya finish the story."

Gēto laughs as well. The children finally stop laughing, and Gēto looks around, then places both hands over his mouth and whispers, "Masutā Asoya."

"This ninja was ruthless, dreaded in the clan he was in because his way of fighting was ravenous 厳酷, but he purposely trained that way."

"I know you can beat this Koroshiya!" Gēto shouts.

Asoya smiles dimly as he looks down at his sheathed sword in front of him. He looks over at one of the workers, then back at the children.

"One day, while on a mission, the Koroshiya encountered a Guardian…"

"What's a guardian? Who are the guardians?" one of the children asks; the child's name was Smiles.

"Guardians are the Angels, silly," a girl named Laughter replies as she chuckles; Smiles chuckles as well.

"Is that right, Mr. Asoya?" Smiles asks.

"Yes," Asoya replies. "The guardians, they are the angels, and the angels are sent from above by God. Now the Koroshiya didn't know that this was an angel. He had never heard of them or seen one before, but they are very real. What he saw was nothing like it. There were other ninjas with the Koroshiya on this mission who had tried to use their weapons to fight against this angel, but all the angel did was wave his hand, and he shattered all of their weapons."

"Wow," the children exclaim along with the workers.

"This angel was protecting someone that trusted in The Almighty One. The ninjas could not harm the man due to the angel; not even the Koroshiya could get to the man that trusted in The Almighty. The angels protect those who trust in God, as it is written in Psalms 91 where it states, 'For he (The Almighty One, God) shall give his angels charge over thee (the command and duty of watching over you), to keep thee in all thy ways.'"

"Are the angels around us now?" one of the workers asks.

"They are," Asoya says, "Even though you cannot see them right now with your eyes, they are there. But we don't focus on the angels, but rather on The Almighty One Himself."

Asoya teaches Elisa, along with the workers and children, how to say the Psalms 91 prayer.

CHAPTER 30

ASOYA TELLS ELISA ABOUT TRANG

THE FOLLOWING DAY, ASOYA RETURNS. WHEN THE children went outside to play, Asoya tells Elisa about his travels and how an unexpected shadow has emerged, a shadow from his past, and this trained shadow's name is the Red Velvet Shuriken.

"Really? Wow, Asoya, it must have been nice seeing your friend again," she says with genuineness, thinking that him seeing a past friend was a pleasant experience for him.

"Nice? A ninja who does things by the law and oaths of the ninja is not nice," says Asoya. " Nice you say, you should tell that to him."

"Wasn't he happy to see you?" Elisa asks with an inquisitive look.

"Oh yes, he was happy to see me. So happy that he took out his sword and tried to talk to me with it. His throwing stars were also friendly, like pudgy little snorting piggies," Asoya says sarcastically as he throws his hands in the air, chopsticks in one hand and a bowl in the other. Elisa covers her mouth as she giggles softly.

"Poor Asoya," she says with sympathy, looking at him with a smile.

"I'm being serious, Elisa," he says frowning, not thinking that Elisa was taking him seriously about the past shadow that has stepped on the scene amidst his journey.

"I know, I know, Asoya," Elisa says with laughter in her voice. Asoya grunts as his arms remain in the air.

"It's just that you are one of the most unique Word Carriers I have ever met or heard of. You were once a ninja whose rankings were the highest as an assassin in his clan, now carrying God's word to the people, bringing them hope."

When this is said, Asoya put down his bowl with his eating utensils, looks at Elisa, and says, "I've been sent on plenty of missions, carrying out the orders that were given to me, but this … this is one challenging obstacle. He was the only family I knew, and though in the clan, we were all taught to be family, he is the one that I considered my brother, not by name but as though were blood-related."

"This is a deep shadow for you, I see," she says with concern. She then looks outside and sees the children running and playing. Not too far behind them were the other workers running with the children as they were all playing.

Elisa looks back at Asoya and says, "Sure, the path that is laid out before you may look tough and have its challenges, but this is why God chose you, because He knows that you can handle it."

When Asoya heard these words, he took his eyes off the bowl of noodles and gazed at Elisa.

"This obstacle would not be so challenging if it wasn't Trang, anyone but him. Send Gekijō again or Pendulum for all I care. My clan's master has sent many mercenaries to pursue me, and I've picked them all apart with ease."

Asoya pauses, then sighs. "And it's troubling you that he is coming to fight against you isn't it," asks Elisa.

Asoya looks down at his bowl, picks it up and starts to eat again. He picks up a large portion of noodles with the chopsticks, brings it up to his mouth, and partakes. He swallows the noodles after chewing them for a while, then reaches for his cup of tea. He does not drink it but holds the small cup at chest level, looking down at it.

"Your friendship or past friendship you had with your brother from the shadows, Trang, is weighing you down." Observes Elisa. "You have enough things that you deal with; you do not need this to add to your load."

"Hey…" he jests as he listens to Elisa.

"I'm being serious, Asoya" she says in a low, firm voice. She was copying Asoya, throwing both of her arms into the air and putting both hands up just as he did earlier. Asoya grins, knowing she was mimicking him and doing so to lighten the mood. He quickly turns his head to the side and looks at Elisa out of the corner of his eyes with solemnity.

"I am only kidding," she says laughing, "I'm just kidding." She then looks serious. "This is what the enemy does."

"The enemy? Ha ha" says Asoya.

"Yes, this is what the enemy does. He brings things back from our past to try to slow us down. First, the enemy tried to slow you down by reminding you of what you once did as an assassin; now he's using your past friendship with Trang."

Asoya listens to Elisa's words and allows them to sink in; he knew them to be true.

"I just pray that the Lord opens Trang's eyes as he did mine to receive the truth."

CHAPTER 31

GROWTH IN THE MIDST OF RAINFALL

AFTER FINISHING HIS TEA, ASOYA PICKS UP HIS BLADE and heads out the door. After five minutes, Elisa remembers that she wanted to give him a present, so she runs to her back room and grabs one of the paintings she was working on, and hurries to catch Asoya. Before leaving, however, she informs the workers that she will not be gone long. Asoya walks slowly, thinking about Elisa's words, and although he thinks, he is aware of the sounds that are around him. He unexpectedly hears dirt shuffling and turns around to see Elisa. Thinking it was an emergency, he asks, "Is everything alright, Elisa?"

After she catches her breath, she nods her head, letting him know that everything was fine. She does not look at him, but only at the painting in her hands.

"I know that you are going through a lot during this time, the time of the rainy season, so I painted this for you. It is the Ajisai flower. Despite the rain and lack of sunlight, it still grows, just like you. I hope that whenever you look at this painting, even though there are showers, mud, and cloudy days, it will remind you that there is still beauty to be seen," she says with a smile. Looking at her painting, she then closes her eyes, bows her head, and extends the painting towards Asoya. "Please take it."

Asoya looks down at the painting, seeing how important it was to Elisa for him to have it. He smiles and then reaches for it, taking it from her hands.

"Thank you," she says with her head still down. She then looks up at Asoya, turns and rushes back to the orphanage.

CHAPTER 32

AKI, THE SEASON OF AUTUMN 秋の季節

IT IS NOW AUTUMN 秋の季節, THE SEASON OF *AKI* and as the seasons change, so have the trees. Asoya makes his way back home, and leaves drift slowly from the trees and land softly on the earth. Shades of yellow, brown, red, and orange cover the ground like a woven blanket. He treads on the top of the newly fallen leaves carefully, trying not to leave a trail as he walks. He is thinking about the art of being still.

Stillness is an art that those who are labeled ninja are proficient and dexterous in—being quiet, unobtrusive, and calm. Whether it be to lurk around a victim or study a certain region and its activities, ninjas are experts in stillness. When one is still, they can hear things that they normally cannot hear, notice subtleties around them and in the distance, whether it be through sound or the slightest of movements.

By being a Koroshiya, stillness means to slow down in such a way that one almost halts their activities, their own movements physically or mentally so that they can hear and so that they can see, thereby focusing better.

When a ninja is in a clan, they receive orders in the form of a document, or map about what mission they are to execute next. Asoya looks up into the autumn sky as he travels and talks to the Lord, saying, "He who dwells in heaven, the maker of all things, you are my Master now, I need orders. I ask you to order my steps. Order my steps in your word." His words reflect the sentiment of Psalm 199:133 and are said with humbleness.

The autumn wind causes his hair to move back and forth lightly. He stops walking to take in a slight gust. His chest flashes red, and golden words flow out of his heart and appear before his eyes. The words are from Psalm 46:10: "Be still and know that I am God: I will be exalted among the heathen, I will be exalted in the earth."

The golden words slowly turn invisible, his chest stops glowing, and so he continues to walk.

"Be still," he says, understanding the Lord's word. Being still as a Word Carrier does not mean not doing anything, but rather, recognizing who God is and what He can/will do in the lives of His people in the earth.

"Yes, Master, for I Asoya will exalt, lift, promote and edify you among the people," he says watching the wind blow and carry the leaves around. He was ordered to continue to abide under a shadow, the shadow of The Almighty. He makes it to his place of dwelling. He leaves his door open to allow a breeze to come through his room; it is soothing against his skin as the wind reminds him of his childhood autumns. He hangs up the painting that Elisa gave him, thinking about what she said regarding seeing beauty despite the rain. After looking at it, he closes his eyes, inhaling and exhaling the autumn air.

"Aki," he says, smiling with his eyes still closed. Aki, in Japanese, means the season of fall, the season of autumn 秋.

CHAPTER 33

AMBUSH 待ち伏せる

HE UNRAVELS A SCROLL AND STARTS TO READ GOD'S word. Hours pass as he reads the same verse over and over. The light outdoors starts to dim, and the shadows close in as it is now evening. After rising to slide shut the open door, he continues to read Psalm 119:80:"Let my heart be sound in thy statutes (ruling, ways, decree, order); that I be not ashamed. Lord...let my heart be sound in your statutes."

He blows out the candle, rolls the scroll back up, then lies down on his mat. He sighs as he continues to think on God's word. He closes his eyes.

"Look at the coward."

"Huh?" Asoya says as he hears whispers coming from shadows throughout his room.

"It's the one who escaped us," one shadow says to another. "Yes, it is he. This is the one who bested Tracker Gekijō."

"What? How did they get in here? How did they find me?" Asoya asks as he eases his hand under his mat, grabbing ahold of a few throwing stars as he had kept a stash under his mat just for the occasion of an unwelcome guest. When he looks up, he sees the room filled with Koroshiya … ninjas … an ambush. He counts twenty-seven trained shadows.

The ninjas laugh and snicker. "Oh, how you have fled, but tonight you will not flee," a voice said from a shadow on the far end of the room.

"We've come to take you back to Master," another voice declares, chiming in close to the center of the room.

"Yaaa!" Asoya shouts as though he were a wild animal trapped in a cage. He did not aim; he just rapidly threw one from his right hand, two from his left, two more from his right hand and five from his left, and three from his right hand. He runs out of stars, so he grabs ahold of his Dai-Kunai 大きなナイフ (large throwing knife) and hurls the Dai-Kunai harder than he did the stars.

"Kei Yahhhh!" he yells as he releases the weapon from his grasp. The large blade smashes into the wall causing it to crack; the Dai-Kunai judders, making a piercing buzzing sound. Asoya's sweat falls as his hand starts to shake, still extended towards the direction he cast the large knife. He brings his hand over his face as he realizes that his room was empty.

It was a dream, a nightmare. Asoya gazes at his blade that is located on the other side of the room. He sighs, gets up, grabs his blade, and then gets back on his sleeping mat. He props the hilt of the sword against his forehead as he starts to quote scripture from Psalm 17:8:"Keep me as the apple of the eye, hide me under the shadow of your wings', Lord, hide me under your shadow."

CHAPTER 34

REFOCUSED RESOLVE

THE MORNING HAS COME. ASOYA WRAPS HIS CLOAK
around himself, then picks up his scarf, wraps it around his neck,
allowing the tassels to drape down the front and the back of his
cloak. He walks towards his front door, past the Dai-Kunai that he
impelled earlier that night. Still resting in the wall, he frowns as he
gazes at it. He briefly looks over at the Ajisai flower painting. He
grabs ahold of his sword, then throws it over his shoulder, allowing
it to rest over his shoulder, and holds it by a string. He slides the
door open, walks out, then slides it closed behind himself.

It was a cool morning but not too cold. Asoya travels for twenty
minutes before jumping into a tree to ward off the trail of anyone
who may have been tracking him. He travels for twenty-five minutes in the trees before returning to the ground. As he walks, he sees
a shadow from the corner of his eye and frantically jumps back,
taking out his dagger. A small wind gush passes by, causing his hair

to sway along with his scarf. He slowly lowers his dagger as he realizes that the shadow he was ready to strike down was his own.

"He, he, he, look at the coward, even his shadows taunt him," Trang says as he watches Asoya from afar.

"Oh, how far you have strayed from the ways of your oaths," Trang says as he pulls his hood over his head, then vanishes into the nearby forest.

"What's going on with me?" Asoya asks as he continues to walk with his dagger tightly gripped in his fist, for he was unsettled and troubled that he would even consider jumping at his own shadow. He was also bothered about the dream he had, a room swarming with assassins, swarming with ninjas.

"I never allowed such frivolous matters to bother me when I was a Koroshiya. Is this because the Lord took my heart of stone out and gave me a heart of flesh as it is written in Ezekiel 11:19? There was a time my heart was stone, but now it is not," he says as he ponders on God's word. Asoya knows better; he knows not to allow such things to get to him. He was trained in the clan to assume nothing but to be ready for anything.

"Anything…" he says, raising his dagger and placing his thumb on the dagger's point, thinking about the clan. He places the dagger away and grabs hold of one of the scrolls.

"Assume nothing, but be ready for anything …" he says, staring down at the scroll in his hand with the word of God written within.

"In the clan, we were taught that one of our own brothers or fellow clan members could one day become our enemy, but I never thought that Trang would come after me or consider me to be his enemy. Then, again, I anticipated nothing less, for Trang was as devoted if not more than I to the clan."

Asoya again looks down at the scroll in his hand and grips the scroll tightly.

"So be it, you are my enemy," he says frowning. "I am no longer ninja, but am a carrier of this Word, and I must continue to carry it doing what candles do best in the midst of darkness."

CHAPTER 35

ASOYA'S MANY TRAVELS

AS ASOYA DID HIS MANY TRAVELS, PEOPLE WOULD often try to give him money. He would thank them for the generosity and tell them, "If you really desire to help, then go and help someone who is in need or who is less fortunate than you."

Many would nod their heads and do just that, but others would insist that he take their Yen (money) 円, which he would, not wanting to offend them. He would take the money others would hand him, then turn around and purchase something for someone really in need. Whether they were poor and needed food, or sick and needed some medicine or just in need of a change of fresh clothing, he used the money to purchase what was needed for them. He did these things and taught others to do the same.

CHAPTER 36

SHORTCUT THROUGH THE KUMOI NISHIKI TREES

ASOYA JOURNEYS TO ANOTHER TOWN, AND ON THE way, he decides to take a shortcut through a small forest. He passes many Kumoi Nishiki trees, a type of maple tree. He looks up at them, viewing the bright red, orange and yellow colors of its leaves. He stops, not because he was marveling at their beauty but because he senses shadows once again. He hears whispers.

"Whispering does not work on one who was once shrouded by the clan. There's more to life than cleaving privately to darkness. Stay your jabbering's, and come out of the shadows," he says knowing someone was watching him.

"And why are you not in the shadows?" a voice says from a shadow still obscured from Asoya's sight; it was a ninja. Asoya speaks nothing but listens carefully.

"But you have chosen to travel in the light where you can be seen, thus making yourself vulnerable to attack 傷つきやすい. Have you confused your night from day?"

Trang was a few yards away, taking refuge in a tree, the thick branches and leaves conceal him as he observes Asoya and listens as he responds to the ninja.

"Everyone who walks the face of the earth was made for the day where the light of the sun can touch his or her skin. Night was made for sleeping...not stalking or killing, but resting. I cannot hide in the shadows any longer, not as long as I carry this," Asoya says to the ninja as he takes out a scroll with God's word contained within.

"In the clan, we are sworn to secrecy. Ninjas are given tasks, and once a job has been undertaken and completed, it cannot be spoken of unless asked by Master himself. Secrecy 秘密. Clandestine. But this word that I carry cannot be held silent; it is meant to be proclaimed. Tell me something, assassin, do you light a candle and put it under a bush or do you set it on a table so that it can give light to everyone that is within that house?"

The ninja does not speak but clings to silence, Asoya continues.

"Again, in the clan, we are instructed to be as shadows and not be seen by those who we prey upon, but in God's kingdom, we are as light because Jesus said that we are the light of the world and light is meant to be seen, not hidden."

Asoya hears whispers, then quietness.

"Who sent you? Did you choose to come after me, or did Master direct you?" Asoya asks as he frowns.

"You did, when you deserted us," the ninja says in reply as he comes out from the shadow he was hiding in, behind a tree. Two ninjas drop from the trees, then four, then six, then four more. They extract their weapons slowly and ease closer to Asoya.

"Let's see what you will do now," Trang says quietly as he leans closer to see Asoya's reaction through the leaves. Like a shark circles its prey and lies in wait for blood, so do the ninjas circle Asoya, but only this prey isn't really prey.

"Open your eyes and see. Count how many ninja have fallen over the years because they were mere pawns to their master's beckoning, only to be discarded as mere objects. This road that you are on is not a road that leads to life, there is a way that leads to life. This road is not it," Asoya says, trying to get through to the ones he was once in the clan with. The ninjas laugh at his words.

"Roads and life? These words are foreign 外国人. Where have you gotten such teachings? We are but tools for the clan and masters will. Only a defector would speak such things, " one of the ninjas blurts out with conviction, pointing his sword at Asoya.

"No, only one who has been redeemed from darkness and stepped into the light would speak such things," Asoya says as he continues frowning.

That was his last statement because he realizes that it is pointless to try to reason with a shark 鮫. One of the ninjas run at Asoya, so he punches the ninja amid his chest and abdomen, and the ninja smashes into the ground like a bag of rocks. Asoya looks up at the other ninja who were ready at any moment to attack him. One down, sixteen remain standing. All sixteen ninja pounce at him.

Asoya kicks a ninja on his talus 距骨, the area between the foot and anklebone that connects the lower leg bones to the ankle joints. The ninja falls, holding his foot. Asoya rams his knuckles into another ninja, hitting his femur 大腿骨, the muscles in his leg that surround the femur went numb so that ninja falls too. Three of the ninja are now on the ground; now, just fourteen remain standing.

"Ruthless Vermilion, what happened to you? I do not recognize you, and your bodily scars, how is it possible that they are gone? I was there when you received most of them," Trang asks under his breath as he thinks about the words Asoya just spoke. Trang then starts to think about how they first met.

CHAPTER 37

THE RAIDING OF A VILLAGE

A YOUNG BOY WAS CRYING ON A STREET CORNER AS the ninjas raided the village he was in.

"Hey…" Trang said to the little boy as he walked up to him. "Don't cry; everything is going to be alright," he said as he patted the young boy on the head. "My name is Trang, and I'm six years old. What's your name?"

"My name is (sniff, sniff) Asoya," the boy said as he tried to hold back his tears.

"Asoya, that's a nice name. How old are you?"

"This many…" Asoya said as he held up four of his fingers.

"Four? Hey, I won't let anything happen to you; I will protect you," Trang said as he extended his hand in Asoya's direction. "Just stay with me."

"Okay," Asoya agreed as he took Trang's hand. Together, they ran off to see the head ninja.

"Where's your mom and dad?" Trang asked Asoya as they ran.

"They left me a long time ago," he said, rubbing his eyes as he continued to cry.

"They left you?" Trang asked, surprised. Trang was taken from his family to be raised by the clan, while Asoya was abandoned by his. This saddened Trang as he started feeling the pain that Asoya felt. Trang walked up to one of the head ninjas and begged him to take Asoya with them. The ninja saw the look in Trang's eyes and granted his request.

Trang comes back to reality as he allows his first memory of Asoya to fade. He turns and continues to watch Asoya battle.

Asoya maneuvers through his attackers untouched, a craftsman, he was still his clan's sharpest point. One ninja remains standing and swings frantically at Asoya with his sword ten times. Asoya kicks the hilt of the ninja's blade, he then spin-kicks the ninja in the back of his head, and the ninja starts to fall. The sword that Asoya kicked out of the ninja's hand soars in Trang's direction.

"What?" Trang says to himself as he sees the ninja's sword jetting his way. The sword went past Trang's head, planting itself into the bark of the tree. Trang turns his head, looks at the sword, and he quickly looks back at Asoya, who is now gone; he has vanished. The ninja's body hits the ground. Trang looks back at the sword; there was a scroll on it. Trang yanks the sword out of the bark of the tree and grabs the scroll that was attached to it. He unravels the scroll and reads it, reciting Matthew 12:30:

"He that is not with me is against me, and he that gathers not with me, scatters."

"Riddles, why do you continue to quote these conundrums? What does this mean?" Trang asks as he continues to read.

"I serve a new Master, and His name is Jesus. Every knee shall bow to Him, even you. Trang. If you are not with Him, then you are against Him, and if you are against Him, then you are against me. For I am one of those who serve Him, and I choose to gather with Him, but you gather not with Him, and this is why you scatter. The clan is no longer my home: the shadows hold no place for me."

"P.S. It's Kingdom stuff, I'll tell you about it later."

"New Master?" Trang asks as he struck the side of the tree with his fist in anger, leaving a deep imprint.

"You dare to the mock the clan and try to separate yourself from us? Claiming a new Master too?" Trang pauses, looking at the ninja laying on the ground. He smiles, then looks at the sword that Asoya kicked in his direction and says, "You've come a long way from the young child crying on the corner of the street."

That night it was hard for Asoya to maintain his stance as a Word Carrier, for the clan (and Trang) press heavily upon his mind.

"Hold up my goings in thy paths that my footsteps slip not. I feel as though my steps are slipping..." he says, quoting Psalm 17:5 as he gazes at both of his hands and then looks up. Asoya cracks the wall with his fist, frustrated that his mind was starting to revert to the ways of a Koroshiya, to the ways of an assassin. For Asoya was just around sharks, and that shark-infested water was familiar to him, for he once swam in the shadows, swimming like a shark. The shark, the Koroshiya, the clan and the ninja…

CHAPTER 38

TEETH AND SHARKS

ASOYA'S ALTERCATION WITH THE CLAN MEMBERS triggers a memory, and this memory was of teeth, sharks, and combatants.

"Sharks are the predators of the sea, but the ninja, the ninja are the real predators 捕食者 of the shadows," Trang said as he trained Asoya.

"What is the shark's ability and main weapon?" Trang asked Asoya.

"Their ability is hunting, and their weapon has to be their teeth," he replied.

"That's right," Trang said. "It is one of the many things that makes them so deadly. Sharks are hunters; there is nothing pleasant about their hunt at all. When they strike, they are savages."

Asoya looked down at his sword and spoke, "This is what makes me deadly."

Trang noticed the way he handled it and looked at his sword. "I'm going to tell you something about the shark's teeth, Asoya. Their teeth are already on their body, in their mouth; it is their weapon."

"What do you mean?" asked Asoya, as he examined the metal on his sword and went over in his mind what Trang just spoke about the sea's natural predator, the shark.

"As a ninja, your weapons are more than the tools you use. Fighting is far more intricate then using your sword; it is combative 格闘. Your feet, fingers, toes, and hands are your weapons; they are already on your body, just like a shark's teeth are already in its mouth. Your sword is just extra. If your natural weapons such as your sword or shurikens are taken from you, you should be just as lethal 残忍な if not more lethal without them. You not having a sword should not dilute your lethality."

Asoya understood. He put his sword down, frowning, and then looked over at Trang. Whenever Trang would go on his missions, he would find valuable scrolls and teachings in certain homes from those who would travel overseas; these scrolls were from other nations such as Africa, Spain, Rome and Greece, and many others. History fascinated him, but above all, those nations and their lethal forms of fighting. There was a scroll he was reading from and studying; this particular scroll that he once found was from Thailand. Featured on the scroll were a few painted figures performing deadly movements.

It was from the art of fighting that is called *Muay Thai* ムエタイ. It was these different moves along with others that he would secretly incorporate into his personal training regiments along with what the clan was teaching him. It was these moves that he would teach Asoya without taking away from the traditional movements and teachings of Japan, the teachings of the ninja.

CHAPTER 39

COMBATIVES

TRANG TAUGHT ASOYA ELBOW AND SHIN TECHNIQUES

肘とすね that he learned from the scrolls that came from ancient Thailand that produced Muay Thai combatants. When Trang demonstrated the moves, Asoya was confused; he did not understand why Trang was teaching him such things.

"Trang, this is not a common move that we are taught as ninjas. What do these movements have to do with being ninja?" Asoya asked after being frustrated due to the moves being so different than what their master, along with the other instructors, taught him.

"I know, Asoya, but this move and many other moves that I will teach you that I learned from the scrolls of Rome, and Greece, and even Africa will put your opponent down quickly 急いで. There are many different styles of fighting. There are several different ways to bring about your opponent's pain 疼痛. If you are ever engaged by multiple opponents challenging you, you should fight in such a way that it embeds fear in the ones who are witnessing you fight, making them think twice about entering your striking range."

Asoya was quiet as he listened; Trang's words made sense.

"Concerning this elbow strike and shin moves, if you have not fought someone from Thailand that practices Muay Thai, then you do not understand pain. They understand pain."

Asoya accepted Trang's teachings and incorporated them with the rest of what he learned concerning fighting. He practiced the elbow strikes, and shin blows on a wood dummy for an entire week.

"I think you're ready," Trang said after he saw Asoya pick up the techniques quickly. There were four ninjas down the hall; Trang saw them, and in less than three minutes, the ninjas would pass by the room.

"Hey!" Trang shouted with a grin. "Asoya said that all of you fight like samurai, pass gas loudly every two seconds, and are not true ninja, ha ha ha! He said your gassy stenches give away your locations when on a mission!" Trang shouted, trying to keep a straight face while laughing.

Asoya quickly stopped striking the dummy and rushed to the center of the room.

"No, I did NOT say that!" he said, but the ninjas were already agitated about such a remark and continue coming their way while mumbling.

"Wait a minute. Brothers, I spoke no such things. We don't fight each other; we're family, FAMILY!"

"Relax, Asoya, just go with it," Trang said as his laughter stopped and was replaced with a smirk as he saw four ninjas walking with intensity into the room they were in. Asoya sighed, closed his eyes, then balled up both of his fists. He then opened his eyes while frowning.

"That's right; you're all less than samurai, you're rōnins, master-less マスターレス," Asoya said to the four ninjas when they made it into the room and were very angry.

"What did you just say to Trang about us?" one ninja asked, demanding an answer.

Asoya laughed. "You heard what I just said, you're all lower than samurai," he said as the laughter left and seriousness gripped him. All four of the ninjas came at Asoya, so Asoya did the moves that Trang taught him on all of them. All four ninjas hit the floor fleetingly, but quicker than any other move that Asoya had done before and less than a minute had passed. One ninja was on the ground holding his own neck, and another ninja was applying pressure on his own ribs, trying to relieve the pain he was feeling. Another one was holding his shins with both hands, and the fourth one was holding his arm. All four were moaning in agony.

Trang looked over at Asoya and unfolded his arms. "As I told you … pain," he said, frowning. Asoya nodded his head as he saw the ninjas on the floor.

"Pain 疼痛," said Asoya, looking down at his elbows and shins.

Trang watched the ninjas who were still on the floor and spoke, "Remorse is not our way; mercy is not written in our creeds. We are sharks."

CHAPTER 40

TRANG LISTENS TO ASOYA SPEAK

The present:

TRANG TREADS UPON THE TOPS OF THE TREES. HE HAS a traditional archery bow アーチェリー in his hand called a *Yumi*. He sees a lake past the trees, does a front flip out of the tree, then rolls on the ground, gets up and continues to run. He takes out a long arrow then slides on his knees, shooting his arrow across the lake. A rope was tied to the arrow he just released, and his knees stops just before reaching the lake. The arrow hits a building. He grabs ahold of the rope, then runs and ties it to the tree. He jumps on the rope and sprints on it as though it were the ground to the top of the building. He cuts the rope, then yanks the arrow out of the building. He sees Asoya talking to a group of people. He sits down on the backside of the roof, remaining hidden, and listens with his back turned to Asoya.

127

"While we were yet sinners, Christ died for us. While we were still in our sins, He gave His life for us," explains Asoya.

"Sins?" Trang asks as he stops carving the nectarine with his gold throwing star, and turns looking down to where Asoya was speaking.

Sins… Trang thinks to himself, then turns and continues to carve and eat the nectarine as he listens to Asoya quote Matthew 4:16 and John 12:46.

> "Before Jesus came, we all sat in the region and shadow of death, and to them who sat in the region and shadow of death, light sprung up. And the light which sprung up was the Messiah, Jesus. Jesus said that he has come as a light into the world, that whosoever believeth on Him should not abide in darkness,"

A man from the crowd spoke, "What is this shadow of death you speak of?"

"Shadows..." Asoya says, as he looks down then up at the man who asked the question. "The shadow in the context of this verse is death. Death abides upon all men because of sin; we are all born into it. For the wages of sin is death, but the gift of God is eternal life."

The man and the people in the crowd continue to listen to him refer to John 4:10 and John 4:19.

"Jesus came to give us eternal life. It is written in his word that before we loved Him, He first loved us."

CHAPTER 41

TRANG REMINISCES

THAT NIGHT, TRANG THOUGHT HARD ON ASOYA AND the words that he spoke.

"Is this why you're going around doing all these good deeds? For atonement?" Trang says in anger. He then takes out his blade and slices down three large trees, trying to make sense of Asoya's betrayal. The trees finally tumble over; the forest bed rumbles as the autumn trees touch the ground. Trang takes out a gold-plated star and casts it at the scroll Asoya left with him that was already pinned up by a dart.

"What was this new Master of yours able to do that we could not? Give you peace?" he asks balling up his fist. "I remember the day in our clan when you fully became a weapon; you were one of our clan's sharpest points."

CHAPTER 42

THE ASSIGNMENT THAT CHANGED ASOYA INTO VERMILLION

ASOYA, TRANG, AND FOUR OTHER NINJAS MADE IT back from a mission they were assigned to together. Trang was nineteen, and Asoya was seventeen. Asoya pulled down the black cloth covering his mouth and nose that concealed his identity and then removed his head covering. "It wasn't easy keeping up with you today," he said as he looked over at Trang.

"Who was keeping up with whom?" Trang asked, "You took out five targets in less than three minutes that were spread out throughout the building. I only took out two."

Asoya chuckled, "Hey, Trang, do you mind showing me more hand-to-hand techniques in the morning?"

"If I showed you more methods, what would I have left in my reserve?"

Asoya smiled. Trang looked at the other four ninjas, then moved his head, signaling for them to leave. They all dispersed, so he then looked again at Asoya.

"You are harsh on the battlefield, but in the clan, you are relaxed. You have to toughen up; you smile way too much."

"I can't help it," Asoya said, looking down at his sword. "I never had a family; you and this clan are the closest thing to a family that I have."

They walked on.

"Trust no one, Asoya, not even me. This is the way of the ninja; we are weapons," Trang said with seriousness. Asoya looked over at him; the smile that was on his face slowly left as he saw the seriousness on Trang's face.

Asoya looked down at the floor. "I understand, trust no one. That leaves one thing for me to trust, my sword," Asoya said with disappointment. He took his sword from its sheath. "I trust in my sword," he said with sincerity.

Trang stopped walking and said. "Asoya, listen to me."

Asoya took his eyes off his sword and turned to look at Trang; he, too, stopped walking.

"You will be the highest-ranking amongst us."

"What?" Asoya asked as he started to laugh. "There are so many ninjas in this clan, plus you are rising in the ranks. The other ninjas call you Red Velvet, the Precise Shuriken."

Asoya's laughter stopped as he was looking down at his unsheathed weapon. He repeated Trang's shadow name. "Red Velvet..."

Trang took out four throwing stars and spun them Asoya's way. Asoya refracted them without looking. Two stars hit the ceiling, and the other two smashed into different parts of the wall. Trang then ran up to Asoya and thrust his sword at him five different times at five different parts of his body, and Asoya's sword blocks all five strikes. It was an automatic response; Asoya does not think at all, it was just reflex for him, and Trang knew this. His blade rattled while the metal on Asoya's sword rang.

CHAPTER 43

A NATURAL GLADIATOR

TRANG LOOKED AT HIS OWN SWORD THEN BACK AT Asoya who was gazing in the distance. Asoya then broke his gaze and looked over at Trang, frowning.

"See what I mean? You are a natural, a Gladiator. You didn't even think, but you just do, and what you do is on impulse, the sign of a true ninja."

Asoya lowered his blade, and so did Trang.

"I'm not kidding, brother, you will be feared amongst the shadows," Trang said, walking up to Asoya as he placed his hand on Asoya's shoulder.

"You are different than the others; it was like you were made for this, a prodigy. What it takes months and years to learn, you absorb in a day, and by a week's time, you have perfected what you were taught. I've never seen anything like it, and your strength is as the strength of three men, and you are just seventeen. If you were

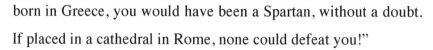

born in Greece, you would have been a Spartan, without a doubt. If placed in a cathedral in Rome, none could defeat you!"

Asoya looked at his sword.

"But, you could defeat me," Asoya said, looking at the deep scar on Trang's shoulder.

"I am your teacher apart from Master, but Asoya, you will surpass even me. No one in the clan wants to spar or even train with you because you would hurt them."

Trang chuckled, and Asoya laughed too, but quietly.

"I don't mean to."

"That's the point, you are a natural at it. You are a Gladiator, Asoya, and our sharpest weapon, you'll see."

A messenger ninja sprinted over to Asoya and Trang's location. He then bowed before Trang and spoke, "Master has a message for you, Red Velvet."

Trang looked serious, and said, "Deliver the message you were sent to dispense."

"He has a solo mission that he wants you to complete before the night is over. He knows that you just returned, but it is urgent."

"I am not tired; my shuriken's burn for their next targets."

"Here is the document," the ninja said, and sprinted off.

"Another solo mission, that's your fifth one so far." Observed Asoya.

Trang covered his own nose and mouth with a black cloth.

"Remember what I said, brother, you will outrank us all," Trang said as he dashed away to complete the task he was given.

CHAPTER 44

INFILTRATOR?

ASOYA ENTERED HIS RESTING QUARTERS, AND AFTER cleaning his blade, he looked at the scars that covered his own body, the majority of them sustained from various missions.

"The highest-ranking? Me?" He lay down on his mat, staring at the ceiling. There was an explosion within the clan.

"An infiltrator 侵略者?" Asoya asked as he got up off his mat and rushed over to retrieve his blade. He was ready; no one makes an attempt on the clan and escapes. He slid his door open, almost knocking it off the wall, and ran in the direction in which the explosion occurred. Heavy smoke was rose from one of the rooms at the far end of the building.

"What happened?" Asoya asked as he ran past a group of ninjas who were not moving with quickness at all.

"It's nothing, just Gekijō again," one ninja shouted.

"Gekijō?" Asoya said as he slowed down, shaking his head in disappointment.

"Always tweaking explosives," he said as he made his way to Gekijō's room. Asoya shouted in the room, calling for Gekijō, but there was no reply, so he entered, covering his nose and mouth to protect his lungs from the smoke.

He found Gekijō on the floor. "Gekijō, are you alright?" Asoya asked as he grabbed his shirt and dragged him outside of the room. He struck Gekijō with a pressure point, which caused him to wake up coughing with his eyes crossed. Smoke was rising from his hair.

"Wow! I feel so ALIVE, but I'm also feeling loopy," Gekijō said, getting up off the floor with Asoya's help.

"Now I know what happens when you mix these two chemicals together," Gekijō said, rushing back over to the room but did not enter.

"Danger," Asoya said as he looked back at Gekijō's room; it was completely destroyed.

"No, it's a beauty. It's so marvelous!" Gekijō yelled, taking out a bomb and rubbing it obsessively then kissing it.

"Something is extremely wrong with you; do you know that?" Asoya asked, as he chuckled. He then patted Gekijō on his back because a small fire was starting to spread across his clothing, so he helped by putting the fire out.

"I need a name, a name that describes me as a ninja, a name that is worthy of the works that I create," Gekijō said as he pointed at his destroyed room, admiring it as it as though it were an expensive painting at an art exhibit.

A ninja, two doors down slid open his door with force and shouted at Gekijō, "You're always causing disruptions. You shattered all the glass that I had in my room from that explosion! That's the eighth time you have shattered something of mine this week!" said the ninja, who then slammed his door shut.

"Shattered?" Gekijō asked as he thought for a moment while still marveling at his damaged room.

"People already know me as the Steel Masked Assassin. But… there is no one badder…" he said, and as smoke continued to rise from his hair, he turned and looked at Asoya.

"I know, call me … *Shatter* 粉々になったガラス," he said with a grin, then exuded with laughter.

CHAPTER 45

THE ASSIGNMENT

ASOYA MADE IT BACK TO HIS ROOM AND SAT DOWN IN the dark on a pillow-like cushion.

"Gekijō wants to be called Shatter. Shatter his name shall be then. It fits him; he's always blowing things up. Out of all of the ninja to set foot on this clan's turf, he, by far, is the craziest. I don't know though, Pendulum is pretty crazy as well; he may have Shatter beat," he said laughing. He then looked serious, thinking about the words that Trang said to him about not trusting anyone. He pulled out a small throwing knife known as a Kunai 日本投げナイフ, from his side and spun it around his fingers. He then got off the cushion he was sitting on and flung the Kunai at his back wall; the wall had large kanjis written on it that said the words *kage ryū*, which translates to the words shadow 影 dragon 竜. The knife landed between the two kanjis.

"Trust no one, Trang said, then trust others I shall not. The only thing I will trust is my blade," Asoya said, walking to his sword and extracting it, taking solace and comfort in the cold steel.

Knock, knock, knock.

He heard a knock at his door; it was subtle but firm enough to get his attention. He opened the door only to see a ninja, a messenger by title within the clan. The messenger kneeled, placed his fist over his chest, then said, "I bear news that is worthy of celebration. You are rising in the ranks. You've been given your first assignment, a solo mission."

"My first solo mission?" Asoya asked. *I've never been on a solo mission before,* he thought to himself. "I am a trained shadow; shadows wield their allegiance to their masters," he said while looking down at his sword. He then looked down at the ninja who was still kneeling on the floor; the ninja's head was down.

"You may rise, brother," Asoya said to the ninja, who slowly got up off the floor.

"What is the mission?" Asoya asked the messenger as he looked at his own sheathed sword.

"A man has found one of our hidden bases that contain our reserved weapons. He is planning to take his findings to a samurai employed by a wealthy family; this family is attempting to raise their status in the political arena, and these hidden weapons will be their bargaining chip. This family has already agreed to pay him for his findings."

Asoya looked down at the ninja and asked if the man was a ninja.

"No, Asoya, he has no association with the clandestine; he is a bystander, a civilian. From what our intel has gathered, he is just a farmer."

"A farmer found this information about our clan's hidden weaponry … interesting," Asoya said as he extracted his sword and looked at its metal.

The ninja nodded, then spoke, "He is leaving early morning tomorrow."

Asoya sliced the air with his sword, and while looking away from the ninja, he spun it as though he were getting ready for an intense battle and examined it.

"He will not make it, for an enemy of the clan and Master is an enemy of mine. Where is this man's location?" he asked, turning back around to look at the messenger.

"The location can be found in here," the ninja said, extending a folded piece of paper that was sealed with the clan's emblem, a dragon. Asoya placed his sword in its sheath then took the folded paper from the hand of the ninja.

"This mission I accept."

The ninja lowered his head, then raised it, saying, "The shadows are our allies."

"The shadows are our ally," Asoya repeated back to the ninja. The ninja arose, congratulated Asoya for taking his first solo mission and then dashed off to deliver a message to Gekijō, now known as Shatter.

CHAPTER 46

THE SCAVENGERS

ASOYA FOLLOWED THE SEMANTICS THE NINJA PRE-sented to him and arrived at the house of the target; it took him three hours to get there. He hid in a shadow, a short distance from the house, gathering his own intel before striking. He observed that the man had a few candles lit. As Asoya hid, he heard faint growling, and it did not come from a person. He turned and looked only to see glowing eyes staring back at him; the eyes didn't move, only stared. He counted thirteen pairs of eyes in total. The eyes that are staring at him came from wolves 狼.

"Wolves, you fluffy pooffy puffs, be gone. I don't have time for wild strays," Asoya said as he turned back around, looking toward the house. The philosophy of ninjas is never to be assuaged but always to complete a mission. The wolves growled more, for they smelled blood, not Asoya's blood, but the blood that was on his sword from his many missions. Although Asoya had cleaned it, the wolves still smelled it. He looked down at his blade, then slowly over at the wolves. They started to show Asoya their teeth as they salivated.

One of the core philosophies of a ninja is to slay and eliminate anything that tries to hinder you from accomplishing your mission, but Asoya does no such thing, for he was not threatened by the wild hunters in the slightest. He felt it would be a waste for him to even draw his weapon against them due to him not being ordered to do so.

He dropped his blade on the ground as he frowned at the wild scavengers. They launched at Asoya before his sword hit the grass. They were fast, but Asoya was faster; he struck them all using four fingers from each hand. Asoya was ravenous 下劣. He dug deep into the wild beasts' fur, digging beneath the muscle, hitting nerves that stopped them in mid-attack, causing them to fall asleep. His strikes were as though he were hungrier than they were. He then tied all of them up.

"Bad dogs. My fangs are far sharper than yours," Asoya said as he walked over to where his sword was and picked it up, adding, "You were not my target."

CHAPTER 47

THE MISSION

THERE WERE FIVE CANDLES LIT IN THE HOUSE. ASOYA took out two stars and threw them into the house; the stars hit two candle flames before hitting the wall. Both candles were still intact, even the wick, only the flames were touched. The man walked over to the two candles, which were placed at opposite ends with three candles between the two Asoya just took out.

"A breeze must have blown them out, but why are only two of the candle's flames out and not all five?" he asked as he examined the candle, holding a small cup of hot tea in his hand. The man saw a star behind one of the candles in the wall.

"Wha ...what...NINJA'S?!" he exclaimed as he dropped his teacup. Before the man could run, Asoya threw the third star into the house. The star hit the man; he fell and struggled to crawl. Trang was at a distance, watching Asoya on his mission. Asoya had no knowledge that Trang was watching him because Trang

147

observed him just to make sure that all went well and to make sure he returned to the clan in one piece. Trang saw Asoya take out a fourth star. As Asoya released the star from his hand, he saw a young boy run to his father's side.

"Daddy!" the young boy, who was no more than five years old, shouted.

"What?" Asoya said as he attempted to grab the star that just left the tip of his fingers. He was unable to grab the spinning star, so he took out another star, staggeringly being greatly perplexed, he aimed to try to counter the one he just threw, but it was too late. By that time, the star had already flown into the house, and it hit the young boy, who then fell over instantly. "No...oh NO!" he said to himself, and with his hand still extending toward the house, the second star still in his hand, his hands started to shake. Asoya pulled the mask down that covered his nose and mouth. He stepped forward, trembling, saying, " I didn't...I didn't mean too. No!" he then said it again a fourth time, but this time, it was just a little bit louder. He ran into the house and fell to his knees before the little boy. Trang also ran toward the house but instead hid behind the door.

"Huh?" Trang said, as he looked through the cracked window from outside. Upon seeing the little boy lying on the floor, Trang sighed and looked down, shaking his head. He then looked at Asoya who was trembling on his knees.

"Nooooo!" Asoya shouted at the top of his lungs with tears in his eyes.

"Asoya …" Trang said in a whisper, feeling Asoya's pain and seeing how broken up he was. It didn't bother Trang that the young one was hit, for ninja were taught to show no sympathy 同情なし and to be as cold as the steel that they wield and as sharp as the stars that they impel. It bothered him to see that it affected Asoya so deeply; it was for Asoya that Trang felt sympathy. Trang stepped back from the window slowly, and after watching Asoya some more, he returned back to base. Asoya was devastated and broken, so he also headed back to base.

CHAPTER 48

NINJA, THE WAY OF THE OMINOUS 不吉

ASOYA LAYS THE STARS HE USED ON HIS TARGET BEFORE his Master.

"You have done well" his Master said once he saw the star and the blood they were submerged in.

There was silence, and with a raspy voice, Asoya spoke, "I have failed you, Master." Asoya got down on both knees and placed both fists on the floor.

"How so?" his Master asked, looking down at Asoya.

"There was a young boy; he was no more than five years of age who was struck by a stray star. He was just a young child. Master, I…" he continued, struggling to get out his words.

"Enough! Put away those meaningless feelings 無意味な気持ち, these sentiments. You are ninja, a weapon! We destroy anyone or anything that gets in our way, and such are the ways of those who dwell in the shadows. Regret is NOT for those who are named weapons, it is only for the *kyojaku*."

Kyojaku means weak, the feeble, and the frail 虚弱.

"The frail? But Master…" he said as he rose, his head turning slowly to look at his Master. Upon seeing the rage in his Master's face, Asoya placed one hand over his chest and bowed himself, saying, "Yes, Master."

Asoya rose to his feet and left his Master's presence, leaving the stars before his Master's feet. Upon exiting the door, Asoya picked up his sheathed blade and headed down the long hall. Trang was leaning against the wall with his eyes closed and his arms crossed, waiting for Asoya. Trang's blue hair covered his face. In one of his crossed arms, he held his sheathed blade. When Asoya passed him, Trang opened his eyes, frowned, and then said, "It's going to be alright, Asoya. The ways of the ninja may be ominous 不吉, but you'll see, what we do is necessary."

Asoya took a few more steps before stopping. When he stopped, he looked down at the ground frowning and gritting his teeth. Asoya's grip upon his blade grew tighter and tighter. The veins in his arm started to bulge, his sheath cracked. He then turned and looked at Trang with an empty gaze.

"Necessary? We are clandestine." Asoya said in a deep, solemn and heavy tone. But though it was heavy, his tone was withdrawn.

"Huh?" Trang said as he looked into Asoya's eyes. Something was different; something was off. Trang saw that something had broken in Asoya. Something had snapped; this was not the Asoya that he once knew, this Asoya was different. Asoya turned his head and continued to walk down the narrow hall. Trang turned his head forward and stared at the opposite wall for a few seconds thinking and then closed his eyes. The memory fades, bringing Trang back to reality.

The present:

"After that day, you became cold and distant, always training, training for the next mission for many years after that. With your blade as your only companion, you had no more need for me. You immersed yourself in darkness and became what the clan now knows you as, Ruthless Vermillion."

Trang lifts his sword into the air; as the light of the moon reflects off the steel, he sees his reflection on his blade, and he gazes into his eyes. He frowns, then sheaths his blade. The metal slides slowly into the sheath before he releases his grip on the handle. *Clink.*

"We shall see how well you fend when darkness becomes your cover again. No one escapes the oaths of the shadows, no one! Not even you, Vermillion."

There was a deep scar on Trang's right shoulder; he received it while on one of his missions. It grieves him when he looks at the scar. He then takes out his blade and slices down another tree in anger.

CHAPTER 49

THE BEGGAR AND ASOYA'S PROCLAMATION

IT IS STILL NIGHT AS ASOYA WALKS BACK TO HIS HOME.
He passes through a small town that cut his travel time in half.

"Could you spare some change?" a man asks as he bows before Asoya.

"Man, lift yourself. There's no need for you to bow to me. Jesus is preparing a place for you in His kingdom where you will no longer face a hunger for food or thirst for sustenance again."

"Jesus, why would he do this for me?"

Asoya tells him about John 14:1–2 and explains to him what it means.

"I'm not worthy," the beggar replies as he attempts to hide his face in shame, feeling unclean from his many days of homelessness. Asoya reads to him many scriptures on what it says concerning the poor and told him that the Lord made him worthy. Asoya stops speaking as he feels something heading in his direction,

153

a small knife came at him from the shadows. Asoya grabs the knife and casts it in the direction it came from. It smashes into a building.

A ninja's face emerges out of the shadows, looks at the knife that was in front of his face, then says, "Your skills have dulled, for you have missed!"

"I didn't miss; I issued you a Keikoku," explains Asoya.

By definition, Keikoku means warning 警告. "A warning from one who was once a shark, and this shark has the power to sink his fangs into your flesh," Asoya says as he stares into the shadow the ninja was hiding in.

"Warning? Ha ha hah!" the ninja laughs jeeringly.

"This is my new assignment, to carry God's word to everyone that I can. You will not prevent me from doing what I was sent here to do. Now scatter," Asoya says as he turns his back and starts to walk in the direction of the begging man. The ninja steps into the shadow. Asoya hears metal shuffling from within the shadows.

"Why do they always insist on doing things the hard way?" Asoya asks as he looks out of the corner of his eye towards the shadow. He then turns to the trembling man and says, "Stay back."

Out of the shadows proceeds a chain with a sickle on its end. Asoya hears the sound of a chain rushing his way. He doesn't even turn; he only ducks and moves to the side whereby the chain and sickle is pulled back quickly into the shadows. It is sent out a second time, and just as the sickle reaches Asoya, he turns quickly, unsheathing his blade, and hits the sickle. The sickle falls to the ground along with the chain that was attached to it. The sharp end plunges into the ground, and as the ninja pulls the sickle back into the shadows, it scrapes the ground pulling up earth.

Just before it reaches the shadows, the sickle is yanked up by its chain, taking a large chunk of earth with it. The sickle and chain are immediately sent out from the shadows; this time, however, Asoya grabs the sickle, catching it where the chain connects to the wood, leading up to the chain. The ninja struggles to retrieve his weapon as Asoya examines the sickle.

"Heh, the *Kusarigama* くさりがま... It has been a long time since I've seen one of those," Asoya says while looking at the sharp end of his enemy's weapon.

Kusarigama/Sickle and Chain

The ninja threw the weighted end of the chain at Asoya. At the end of the kusarigama, there was a small weight so that the ninja using it would have a firm grip upon the chain when it was cast or thrown at an enemy. Out of frustration, the ninja throws the weighted end of the chain at Asoya due to him not being able to retrieve the sickle. Asoya sees the weight with the rest of the chain trailing behind it, so he drops the sickle, then places his other hand on the bottom half of his blade handle. The weight closes in. With both hands gripping his blade, Asoya swings downward hard, hitting the weight out of the air. The ninja could feel the gust from the power of Asoya's swing. The ninja rolls out of the shadows and lunges at Asoya. When Asoya looks up, he sees the ninja flying in the air towards him with his hand extended in his direction. The ninja blew on his hand, and deadly powder proceeded from it. Asoya moves out the way avoiding the poisonous powder, then knees the ninja in his stomach.

The ninja falls to the ground, rolls, then yanks his sword out of its sheath. The ninja came at Asoya with a blade in one hand and a dagger in the other while Asoya drew out his blade. The ninja swung twice at Asoya, who dodges the first two attacks. Asoya swung his sword with such tenacity that it knocks the ninja's dagger from his hand; the ninja swings his blade a third time, the third attack Asoya caught with his blade. The blade echoes as his blade met with the ninja's blade.

CHAPTER 50

VERMILLION THE RUTHLESS?

AS ASOYA FORCES THE NINJA'S BLADE OFF HIS, THE
ninja quickly reaches within his garment and pulls out another
dagger. He slices Asoya in the arm, then rolls to the side. As the
ninja rolls, he comes at Asoya for a fourth attack. Asoya swings
his sword the same time the ninja swung his. *Clang* ガラガラ! The
sound of broken metal chimes and overpowers the noise that was
going on around them as Asoya's sword cuts through the sword
of the one who was at odds with him. His sword cut through the
ninja's blade not because it was sharper, but because his swing
contained more malice than that of the ninjas.

"What?!" the ninja exclaims as he gazes at his broken sword.
Shards of metal fragments hit the ground.

"Keikoku 警告," Asoya says with a grimace, and while looking
down at the metal fragments from the ninja's sword, he then looks

over at the ninja. *Keikoku ...warning*...the ninja thinks to himself, for the ninja was in shock.

"I told you, I will not be stopped. You will not prevent me from doing what I was sent here to do. Now, here's a message I have for you: repent 悔い改める."

The ninja says nothing but is shaken, still gazing at his damaged weapon.

"Stop using the shadows to prance on those who have no means of escape and do good. It is time to live in the light, where all your deeds can be plainly seen, and again, I say, do good. Life is being offered you this night, eternal life, and this life can be found in God's Son, Jesus the Messiah. It is time to leave the ways of the shadows and learn the ways of those who walk in the light. Jesus is the True Light that gives light to all men. Learn from Him."

The ninja threw his last star at Asoya, who lifts his sword. The star hits the metal of Asoya's sword, then falls to the ground.

"So, that's your answer," Asoya says as the grip on his blade tightens. "So be it."

The ninja had nowhere to run. There was no escape, for he remembers in that moment who Asoya was, and he knew there was no escaping his clasp; once Asoya's gaze was fixed on you, it was to your ruin 破滅させる. A ninja who was trained to know no terror, experienced it as he looks into the eyes of Asoya who is well known in the clan as Vermillion the Ruthless. Asoya lifts his sword above his head. The ninja closes his eyes, feeling the

159

wind rush past his face, yet there is silence. The ninja opens his eyes only to see a scroll with God's word lying before him. The ninja looks around. "What?" he asks as he tries to find Asoya. Not seeing him anymore, he feels a sense of relief, so he goes over to the scroll, picks it up and escapes into a shadow.

As Asoya sits in the dark in the room that he rented, God's word was spread out before him, lying on a thin cloth. Asoya raises his head, looks forward, and recites Psalm 17:8: "Keep me as the apple of the eye, hide me under the shadow of your wings, under your wings."

Asoya takes comfort in the Lord with that passage. The next day, Asoya goes to the marketplace and convinces one of the workers to give the beggar a job. Asoya found where the beggar was resting, woke him and said the inn keeper agreed to allow the beggar to stay in the room he was staying in for five months, which should be enough to help him get on his feet. Asoya gave the man some money and told him that if spent it on gambling or sake, a Japanese form of alcohol, that he would find him.

The man remembered how Asoya handled the ninja the night before and knew not to disappoint such a man who could over-throw an assassin. Asoya helps the man to his feet and takes him to a restaurant for breakfast. Over breakfast, Asoya continues to share Christ, and tells the man about all the wonderful miracles Jesus performed while he walked the earth.

End of *Asoya*: **Shadows From the Past:**
Trang (忍者、ヒットマン) Section 2

忍者、ヒットマン
Section 3

The Apprehension, the Battle, and the Deliverance

キャプチャー　　　　戦い　　　　　救出

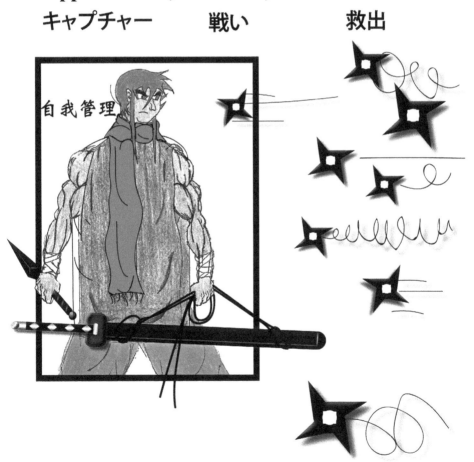

CHAPTER 51

NINJA AND STILLNESS 静止

STILLNESS IS A TECHNIQUE THAT VERY FEW LEARN TO master. There is a group, however, that has mastered this technique and adopted it as part of their training regiments. This group, this organization of trained shadow inhibitors, is known as ninjas. Many different types of ninjas can be identified in different classes. There are spies who gather information either from up close or from a distance. Undercover agents, these can be hidden in plain sight, and one would not know it. There are foot soldiers, trackers, and many other titles. Then, there are those who specialize in hits, and these are known as the hitmen or contract killers, the Koroshiya ヒットマン.

One must be cautious of any of these titles surrounding the ninjas, particularly those that are called hitmen, for they, above all else, cling to the ways of stillness. Stillness when it comes to being a ninja is more than the halting of movements, but calculations 計算

, or assessing any given environment or situation and making calculations accordingly. Calculations on what to do, on what moves need to be made, whether to act or sit still, what weapons would be best for the job, and how long it will take to infiltrate the desired target's location without being noticed. Calculations, like being a shadow, is one of the ninjas sworn techniques and is the perfection of stillness.

CHAPTER 52

READINESS AND AJISAI

"SHARKS ARE INTERESTING HUNTERS 猟師 WITH THE WAY they go after marks. A shark can hurdle forward immediately on its targeted meal if it wants to, but there are times when they circle their prey, warning them that they are near. A Keikoku 警告…is a warning just before they strike, but keep in mind, they will eventually strike," Asoya says as he watches the tools that are before him; these are the tools that he learned to use when he was a Koroshiya. The throwing star—also known as shuriken—the kunai, the sai, the katana, and the *tekkō kagi* which were originally used as tools for farming. The *kakute*, and a few other weapons that are familiar to ninjas, cause him to look up at the wall where his Dai-kunai was impelled after he woke up from a night terror, thinking that he was surrounded by former clan members or assassins, the sharks.

"The teaching of a Koroshiya is to always be ready, just like the shark is ready and familiar with the water that is around it, sensing even the slightest vibrations or movements in the water. I, too, am familiar with the ways that assassins move," he says as he rises off of the wood floor. His attention is no longer upon his weapons.

He walks over to a wooden mannequin that Hedioshi Fukamachi crafted for him for the purpose of training. Asoya strikes it twice using his shins, he then elbows the mannequin once on its shoulder, and the wood splits down the mannequin's arm. Asoya was ready to strike it yet again using his elbow but seeing the painting that Elisa painted for him; his elbow stops as he stares at the Ajisai flower あじさい. He feels a sense of peace. He lowers his elbow. The painting reminds him that there is still beauty to be seen and growth to be done despite the heavy rainfall and what he is going through.

"Beauty and growth," he says in a calm tone, remembering Elisa's words about the Ajisai.

CHAPTER 53

NOZOMI ORPHANAGE

AFTER MUCH THINKING, ELISA DECIDES TO NAME THE orphanage *Nozomi* because Nozomi means *hope* 望む. Asoya tells her that the name was fitting due to her bringing hope to so many little ones. After helping her build a sign with the words Nozomi painted on it and placing it close to the roof a few feet above the door, he sits down and teaches the children.

"There was a man I knew whose name was Gekijō, but many knew him as Shatter," he says.

"Shatter? What kind of name is Shatter?" a young girl named Laughter asks as she and the other children laugh with her.

Asoya chuckles then says, "Shatter was the name given to Gekijō or should I say, Shatter was the name that Gekijō gave to himself, and others called him that because it fit his character. It actually described what he did; he shattered things, broke things, destroyed things. Shatter really was a dragon," Asoya says as he stares off into the distance as though he was in a trance. Smiles, which is the name of another young girl, gets up, walks over to Asoya, and taps him on his knee.

"Mr. Asoya, are you okay?"

Asoya shakes his head, smiles, then says, "Yes. I am alright, thank you, Smiles," as he pats her on the head. Smiles smiled and then went back to her spot on the floor, crosses her legs and places her hands under her chin as she props her elbows up on her knees, eager and ready to continue listening to his story. "Shatter built his foundation and way of life on the sand 砂, and I built mine upon the rock 岩.The sand can represent the world and sin, and the rock represents God. Many people build their lives on the sand, but it is much better to build your life upon the foundation of God. I was once like Shatter, so I know what it's like to live your life on sinking sand."

"You were once like him?" a boy asks.

"Yes, I used to break and destroy things too, but Jesus stepped in and changed me. He pulled me out of the sinking sand and set me upon a rock."

"Wow," say all of the children in unison.

"I tried to tell Shatter about the Lord who is The Rock 岩 and how He can take you out of the sand because who wants to live their life on sinking sand? Who wants to build their life and foundation upon something that is unsteady, only to have it all sink?"

"Did he listen?" Gēto asks.

170

"No."

"So, what happened to him?" a young girl asks.

"He sank."

"How?" Laughter asks.

"He, he, (Asoya laughs) by falling through the floor."

Asoya and all the children laugh.

"Hmmm …" Trang says quietly, as he placed his hand upon his chin, understanding Asoya's message.

"So, this is the word you carry …" he speaks as he looks up into the sky. Trang adjusts his sword, the metal inside of the sheath makes a faint clicking sound, and Asoya hears it, for his hearing is sharp, like that of a newly sharpened throwing star.

CHAPTER 54

FOUNDATION OF THE ROCK 岩

THAT SOUND CAME FROM OUTSIDE OF THE WINDOW, Asoya muses as he grabs his blade and then rushes outside. No one was there. The spot where Trang once sat is empty. *That sound came from right here,* Asoya thinks with watchfulness as he looks at the place he heard the noise travel from. His hand was ready, ready to extract his steel, in case it was a ninja that was near.

"What's wrong, Asoya? Is everything alright?" Elisa asks as she makes it to the front of the house when she notices his hands.

"Yeah," he replies as he moves his eyes around, looking cautiously at his surroundings.

"It was just a bird," he says as he turns and enters the orphanage. Trang peers around the tree a distance away, then vanishes. Asoya goes to the backyard to get some quiet and alone time to think, but the children follow him. He turns around to see large eyes and small faces staring at him.

"We want to hear more about the sand and the rock," Smiles says.

"Yeah, pleaseeee …" they say randomly as they surrounded him.

"Alright, alright," he says as he took out a few throwing stars.

The autumn leaves are falling slowly from the tree that's behind Asoya, so he told all the children to back up. Asoya backs up as well and throws a star at a drifting leaf, pining the leaf to the bark of the tree.

"Wow, that was so cool! Do it again!" Gēto says as he jumps up and down with delight.

As Asoya throws stars at falling leaves, he continues to teach.

"We must build our lives and everything we do upon the rock; we must build our lives upon God."

In between Asoya talking, he throws another star, embedding another leaf into the bark of the tree.

"While Jesus walked the earth, before he was received to glory, he gave us teachings; in His Word, He taught us how to build our lives upon God." When Asoya says this, he throws another star; this time, the star catches a brown-reddish leaf and once again hits the bark of the tree.

"If we build our lives upon the things that God has taught us in His Word, and the teachings of Christ that He gave us, then we will stand," he says while throwing another star. "Jesus talked about he who hears these sayings of His and does them; the key is actually doing what you hear. But he who hears these sayings of His and does them, He likens him to a man who has built his house upon a rock."

He pauses, then turns to the children and asks, "Who is the rock?"

"God!" they all say.

He smiles, turns around and throws three more stars at falling leaves.

"But he who hears these sayings of mine and does not do them, I will liken him to a foolish person who has built his house upon the sand."

"But what's wrong with building on the sand?" a little girl asks, causing a young boy to look over at her and respond, "The sand is not a strong foundation; you can slip and slide on it."

"Oh," she says giggling, understanding why it's not wise to build one's life or house upon the sand.

"Notice that both people heard God's word; one did what they heard, the other did not. Be a doer of God's word," Asoya says throwing the last star.

"Wow," the children say as they saw what Asoya did. He made a large smiley face with the leaves on the bark of the tree.

財団

Foundation

闇

Darkness

> **Whosoever comes to me, and hears my sayings, and does them, I will show you to who he is like: He is like a man which built an house, and digged deep, and laid the foundation on a rock...**
>
> **(Matthew 7:24)**

光

Light

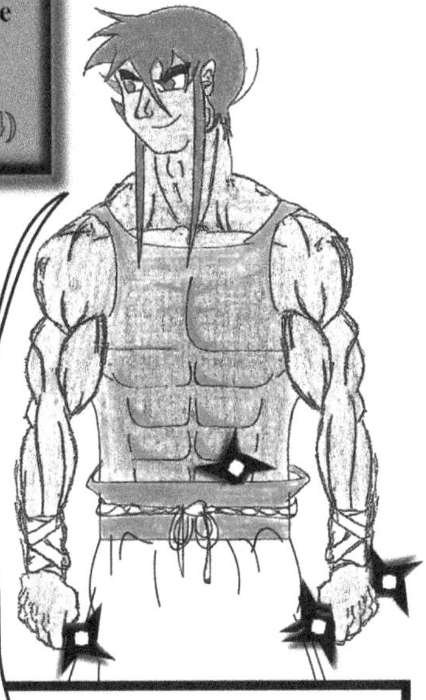

There was a *Ninja* named Shatter whose foundation or life was not built upon the Word of God...and because of this he fell.

砂の基礎
そして石
財団

CHAPTER 55

GĒTO INSTRUCTOR

ASOYA WOULD OFTEN TAKE GĒTO WITH HIM ON errands to show him the importance of serving others and helping those who are in need. He would tell Gēto about the rewards the Lord has for those who labor for Him, and what Gēto learned, he would share with the other children.

"Love," Asoya would tell him frequently, "we do these things not because we have to but because we love the Lord and desire to do those things that please Him."

Gēto would smile as he listened to Asoya, taking in everything he said.

CHAPTER 56

THE SHOWERING RAIN OF METAL

ASOYA GOES INTO TOWN WITH GĒTO TO PURCHASE food for those who need it, as well as for the Nozomi Orphanage. Asoya carries two large sacks of rice on his shoulder while Gēto carries the fruits and vegetables in a bag. As they walk, a star flutters past Asoya's head.

"Assassins," Asoya says, dropping the two sacks of rice. He pulls out his dagger and hits a second star as it flew at him.

"Gēto, go run and hide, and do not come out."

"But…" Gēto starts to argue.

"Go, and when it is night, I will find you," Asoya insists. "Repeat Psalm 91:1 over and over until I arrive. What does it say?"

Gēto hesitates, then says quickly, "He that dwelleth in the secret place of the Most High shall abide under the shadow of the Almighty."

"Say it again, Gēto, this time with confidence," Asoya instructs.

"He that dwells in the secret place of the Most High shall abide under the shadow of the Almighty!"

"Good," Asoya says with a smile. "Now, go run and hide."

"But how will you know where I am?" Gēto asks.

"I will find you," Asoya says as he reaches into his side pouch and takes out a dart 伝統的なダーツ, throwing it in the direction of the ninjas. He hit a flying star out of the air using his dagger. The dagger sparks as the star hits the ground. He turns and looks at Gēto, who understood his message and runs, blending in with a crowd of other people running.

Asoya also runs and hides behind a building. He ties his blade to his back, then takes out his dagger, crossing his arms with a dagger in one hand and a throwing dart in the other to ready himself for the attack. As he looks around the corner, a star smashes into the wall, then soon another. He quickly turns with his back against the wall. One of the scrolls he was carrying falls to the ground unraveling. A few of the words start to glow gold and shine from the page. He picks the scroll up and quickly places his back against the wall again; he looks at it and read the glowing words from Psalm 46:10, "Be still and know that I am God: I will be exalted among the heathen, I will be exalted in the earth."

His heart flashes red as words, written in Hebrew appear on his chest: "לב בדיקת" from those words, more words proceed from his chest, rise upward and flash before his face that read: "Be still. Be still and know that I am God. Be still."

"Be still?" Asoya asks as more stars smash into the wall behind him. He rolls up the scroll and brings his dagger up to his mouth, placing the dull end of the back of the blade inside his mouth and biting it.

He puts away the dart and then climbs the building. He was climbing to get the ninjas to aim high, and aim high they did. When he reaches the top, he takes the dagger from his mouth and sprints across the tile roofing. All he has to do is clear the tops of four buildings (the one he was dashing across made five) before he could escape their grasp. As Asoya runs across the rooftop, he ducks, swerves and jumps as stars pass him.

He uses his dagger to move a few stars away from him; the rest he avoids. A few times, his eyes light up gold as the word he was carrying protects him from the oncoming stars. He jumps off the first building and rolls as he hits the second. He pushes himself up. A ninja climbs the building, but Asoya hits the ninja on his calf muscle using a dart and then trips him, making him fall off the building. The ninja has a rope tied around himself, so as he falls, Asoya throws two more darts down at him, hitting him in both arms causing him to not be able to climb back up again. Asoya then ducks as another star spins by him.

He throws a dart in the direction they are flying from, and it hits one of the nine ninjas throwing the stars, the ninja falls. Asoya continues to run and jumps off the second roof towards the third, and as he glides across the air, stars continue to sail. He blocks four and swipes the fifth one with his dagger. He crashes on the top edge of the rooftop hands first, when he starts to slip. He stabs his dagger on the rooftop, and his feet dangle as he pulls himself up. He exhales, listening to the sound the stars make as they cut through the wind passing him by. He looks up only to see five ninjas awaiting him.

Asoya could jump off the building and land in a wagon below that is filled with hay to catch his fall, and run across the dirt ground, but he chooses not to jump. Instead, he stays on the roof because five ninjas have dared to challenge him. Asoya plows through the midst of them and stops himself before falling off the roof. Turning and facing the direction of the ninjas, he raises his dagger to chest level. Four ninjas fall from the nerve strikes that Asoya hit them with whenever he sprinted past them. One remains standing. The ninja looks about and sees that four have fallen. He turns and looks at Asoya, who glares at the ninja and then raises his left hand in the ninja's direction as though to welcome him to try to test him. Asoya's dagger remains in his right hand at chest level; he is ready 今か今か.

The ninja runs shouting while Asoya bends his arm back with the dagger in it. As the ninja runs with his sword behind him, the ninja quickly raises his sword above his head, then swings it down. Asoya brings his arm forward and slightly upward with his dagger clenched tight in his fist, CLASH 衝突! Asoya's dagger smashes into the ninja's sword. Asoya had swung his arm with such weight that the ninja was pushed backwards and starts to tumble, roll and slide. Asoya remains unmoved in the same spot he stood.

Asoya runs at the ninja who is still sliding, then jumps in the air. While in the air, Asoya heaves two darts at the ninja; however, the darts only tear through the ninja's clothing. For the darts Asoya just threw were only meant to be a distraction 流用. The ninja is in shock, thinking that he is hit, but once he realizes he is not hit, he gets up. When the ninja rises, he lifts his head only to see a foot coming down above him. Asoya's foot falls, meeting the ninja's face. He sighs as he looks down at the ninja, then turns and runs, jumping from the third roof to the fourth.

CHAPTER 57

THE POMEGRANATE AND FALLEN TREE

ASOYA CONTINUES TO RUN, FIGHTING HIS WAY
through an onslaught of stars and ninjas; when he makes it past
the fifth roof, he runs towards the forest to lead any of the stray
ninjas away from the people. After running for some time through
the forest, he stops to catch his breath when he hears a voice
behind him.

"It doesn't have to be this way," a man says.

"What?" Asoya replies as he turns around quickly after being
startled. He sees a man in a hood sitting under a tree in a relaxed
position eating a pomegranate ザクロ. The hood hides the mans
face from Asoya's sight.

"Who are you? Reveal yourself!"

The man takes another bite from his fruit, chews and swallows,
then replies, "All you have to do is turn yourself in, and all of this
will cease."

"Trang," Asoya says, realizing who the hooded man was. Trang waves his finger at Asoya in disappointment and then says, "My name is Red Velvet."

Trang takes his attention off Asoya and grins as he assesses the fruit in his hand and takes another bite. Asoya reaches to his side and slowly draws out his dagger.

"Oh, you're gonna need more than that in just a minute," Trang says as he spits out a few of the seeds from the pomegranate. Asoya looks around, waiting for an envoy of stars from trained ninjas to cascade in his direction.

"Last chance; return to the clan with me, and the atrocities you have committed will be absolved 免除された," says Trang.

"I said it before, and I will say it again: I refuse to walk in the ways of the clan's shadow; I walk in the light now. The ninja who the clan called Vermillion the Ruthless is no more."

Trang shakes his head, gets up and drops his fruit, stepping on it. Turning to the side, he says, "That's sad to hear. Defiance has become your chosen vesture."

He then takes out five gold-plated stars and pitches them at Asoya. As Asoya was blocking the stars, Trang unsheathes his blade and slices the tree that he was sitting under in two. Asoya rushes to attack Trang, however, Trang stands with his arms folded, awaiting Asoya's pursuit. Trang then grins as he takes off the hood that was covering his face and point up to the top of the tree.

Asoya stops and quickly looks up. When Asoya looks up, Trang elbows the tree that was behind him, causing it to slide from its foundation. The tree begins to slowly slide apart in the area where Trang sliced it. Asoya sees that the tree, which is massive in size, about to fall upon the home of a villager.

"No," Asoya shouts leaping into the air and bounces off a nearby tree that was close to him. As he is in the air flying towards the falling tree, he draws out his blade and cuts the tree in three separate places, kicking each part in three different directions and stops it from landing on the nearby home. When Asoya lands on the ground, the hitman named Red Velvet is gone. There are many shadows being cast in the woods that Asoya is in, all of these trees have varying shades of leaves reminding him that it is autumn. Asoya hears a slight whisper echo through the leaves, saying, "Beware my shurikens 手裏剣に気をつけて."

CHAPTER 58

SEVEN HOURS LATER

IT WAS NOON WHEN ASOYA AND GĒTO WENT INTO town to go to the marketplace. Seven hours have passed, the sun was starting to lower behind the clouds. Gēto found his hiding place under a house. He found this spot because he noticed that the boards were loose, so he pulled the boards apart and climbed in. Once he was under the house, he closes the boards behind himself, placing them back where they were.

He remained there the whole seven hours, quoting Psalm 91 as he was instructed. He falls asleep and awakes to hearing the boards move. Gēto backs up, scooting on the ground only to see two eyes staring back at him. He hears a voice …

"It's alright, Gēto. It's me."

"Masutā Asoya!" Gēto says with relief and joy, knowing that Asoya would find where he hid.

"I told you I'd come and find you," Asoya says with a smile.

Gēto also smiles. Asoya extends his hand, Gēto grabs hold of it so Asoya can pull Gēto out from under the house and set him upon his feet. Asoya then puts the boards back in place.

"I apologize that it took so long. I had to wait until it was safe before I could come and find you."

"I know," Gēto replies, understanding why he took so long. Asoya looks around, making sure the coast was clear.

"I got kind of hungry so I ate some of the food," Gēto says looking up at Asoya.

"It's alright. Let's go," he says as he pats Gēto on the head and continues looking around. Gēto notices Asoya's seriousness and imitates him. Asoya senses movement, and from his peripheral vision, he sees something whirling their way, *a shuriken!* he thinks as he yanks his sword from its sheath and hacks the oncoming object out of the air with his sword. He signs once the object touches the ground. It was no shuriken, but merely a leaf that was being carried by the wind.

"Beware my shurikens," Asoya repeats with a mutter as he looks around with uncertainty remembering the words he heard Trang utter during their faceoff after he vanished.

"My Masutā, are you alright?" Gēto asks as he too looks around with hesitancy, mimicking Asoya's every move.

"Stop calling me Master, boy," Asoya says as he sheaths his blade. They continue walking. They make it back to the orphanage.

CHAPTER 59

A NINJA'S SIGHT AND PERCEPTION 感知

"WHAT HAPPENED?" ELISA ASKS, LOOKING AT ASOYA.

Gēto jumps in front of him and says, "Well, I played hide and seek, but I fell asleep in my hiding spot, and Asoya came and found me. He found me because he's a Masutā."

"Okay," Elisa says while getting down on her knees and wiping the dirt from Gēto's face. She then hugs Gēto while Asoya takes the rice sacks and the bag of food and places them in the kitchen.

"It's not safe for me to be here, Elisa, I must leave for a while," Asoya says abruptly but with kindness.

"Why, why, Asoya? You've been doing so well, and the children...they really love you."

"It's not safe! If I could find prey who fell victim to the tip of my blades steel, then surely Trang can trace me back to here, for he taught and he trained me." Asoya says as he sees a woman working

187

that he's never seen working at the orphanage before, points in her direction and asks, "Who is she?"

He sees that the young woman he is pointing to is walking with a limp.

"Oh, her, she just started working here two days ago."

"Two days ago? You can't trust her Elisa, it's a trap."

"Oh, Asoya, not everyone is an enemy. There are actually still good people who—" says Elisa.

"The way of ninja is ominous, Elisa. A true Koroshiya (Assassin/hit-man) knows this, and is always at the ready," Asoya says as he walks over to where his blade was and picks it up.

"Koroshiya? Asoya, you are no longer ninja but—"

"Ninja … no longer Koroshiya, you say? Then why does my past continue to pop up? Is it to remind me of what I once was?"

"Because the Lord—"

"No. No, Elisa," he says as he interrupts her. He then rushes into the room where the young woman is with Elisa tagging behind him. A teaching and philosophy of ninja is to be careful 慎重, and one of the best ways to do this is to trust no one. The young woman is washing dishes and is about to prepare the meal for the children. He walks up behind her to ask, "Who are you?"

The woman turns around, startled, then smiles and says, "My name is—""

"No!" Asoya says, cutting her off. "What clan do you claim? Did Red Velvet send you?!"

"No. Red Velvet who? No, I don't understand you."

"Okay, Asoya, that is enough; you're scaring her."

Asoya unsheathes his blade and says, "Don't lie to me," he points his blade at the woman. When she sees the blade being extended in her direction, she starts to cry and tremble.

"If you harm anyone here—Elisa, the other workers, or any of these children—I will end you. Do you hear me?" Asoya threatens the woman.

The woman falls to her knees as she starts to cry harder. Elisa gets in between Asoya and the young woman.

"Asoya, stop it!"

"Stand aside, Elisa; she's lying!" he says as he grits his teeth while his eyes are still fixed on the young woman.

"That's enough!" Elisa says with tears in her eyes as she gets on the ground with the young woman and puts her arm around her to provide comfort. Asoya looks at the young woman, then at Elisa, then at his blade being extended in their direction. He drops his blade and stares at his hands as he backs up slowly. He then runs out of the house.

"Oh, Asoya..." Elisa says with tears in her eyes.

The children and the other workers surround Elisa and the young woman, putting their arms around them and crying. Gēto stares at them from a distance, wondering. He was trying to comprehend what just occurred when he goes over to where Asoya dropped his blade, picks it up and sheaths it. He props the blade gently against the wall and stares out the open door into the night in the direction Asoya ran.

"Master Asoya …"

CHAPTER 60

SHADOW COMBAT

ASOYA GOES TO A WELL-HIDDEN SECRET WATERFALL

that was behind a mountain. He would bathe there from time to time when he first went into hiding from his clan. He removes his shirt and footwear and washes the wounds that are on his body. He gets into the water, allowing his body to soak. He thinks on Elisa's reaction to him, not understanding why she couldn't see what he saw, or perceived what he perceived 感知. It saddens him that he caused Elisa to shed tears. The water was cold, but the coldness does not faze Asoya. He closes his eyes and listens to the water crash in the background. After he bathes, he places herbal medicine that comes from plants on his wounds. He dresses and then examines all of his weapons. Asoya has an urge to fight and to train.

There was noise, but it came from the gentle flow of water that fell from the cliff above. There was hardly any light in that hidden space, but he does not need it. He takes out his dagger, it echoes throughout the enclosed area, evoking movements that are not for play, but for harm …shadow combat 影の戦闘.

Asoya's feet move across the stony, sandy, and rocky ground. Though his feet move, they do not make a sound. The only noise that is made is coming from his dagger and throwing stars in his hands as they cut across the air. His dagger spins, flails and slices like a wild tempest ワイルドテンペスト. There was no beauty in his movements, nothing graceful, just potency with each attack, a mutiny that was geared and aimed towards the clan. Anything that got before his swing in that moment would instantly be severed, leaving nothing and no one standing. Thus is the way, philosophy, thinking and mindset of those that are called ninjas 忍者.

"For the ways of a ninja are the ways of the ominous," Asoya says, pointing his weapons at the shadows.

CHAPTER 61

MEDITATIONS 瞑想する

WHEN ASOYA LEAVES THE HIDDEN SPOT AND MAKES IT back to his dwelling place, there is no light on in the room, only shadows and quietness. It is in this place that Asoya sits. He meditates 瞑想する as he always has done, but not on the scrolls that contains God's word; he meditates on the ways of an assassin instead. He sits with his eyes closed and fists in his lap, cleaned dagger on the floor in front of him, and his throwing darts surround him, reminding him of what he was forged for. In his meditation, he pictures forty ninja pursuing him in the night. He imagines not escaping from them but putting them down permanently.

He throws darts at each of them from different shadows undetected and unnoticed 未検出. There is one ninja left, but before he imagines throwing the final dart, his chest flashes red. He opens his eyes and grabs his chest as though he were in pain. He looks down and sees Hebrew words 'לב בדיקת' which being interpreted means 'heart check' or 'heart examination'.

"Master, these are ninja," he says looking up at the ceiling. "They are after me, I must protect myself, besides that Trang …"

Before he utters more words, one of the scrolls in his room starts to glow, getting his attention. He looks over at it, and it unrolls, words rise off the page and float over to where Asoya is seated. The words came from Exodus 20:13 which read: "Thou shall not kill."

"These are not normal people," Asoya says calmly and with a sad expression. "These are assassins, and not just a few but a regiment, a squad of trained mercenaries, I have to protect myself and those who I care for."

Another scroll moves and words rise off the page, glowing transparent gold as they float over to Asoya like a feather. These words came from Psalm 91:1-4. As they move before his face, he reads them.

"He that dwelleth in the secret place of the Most High shall abide under the shadow of the Almighty. I will say of the LORD, He is my refuge (my safe place from harm or danger) and my fortress (my fortified defense structure): my God; in him will I trust. Surely, he shall deliver thee from the snare (trap) of the fowler (hunter, a person who hunts), and from the noisome pestilence."

More words from 2 Corinthians 5:20 glow before his face that read:

"Now then, we are ambassadors for Christ (His representatives on the earth), as though God did beseech you by us: we pray you in Christ's stead, be ye reconciled (restored, reunited and joined) to God. For he hath made him (Jesus) to be sin for us, who knew no sin; that we might be made the righteousness of God in him."

"An ambassador 大使," Asoya says, understanding the words. Exodus 20:13 flashes before his face again, "Thou shall NOT kill."

Asoya picks up a throwing dart, then sets it down quietly. He hears a gentle voice refer to Psalm 91:1 and John 15:4 on the inside of him that says, "Abide in me …dwell in me…"

"Yes, Master," he says as a calm overtakes him. The words that flashed before his face start to slowly float around his body, then one by one, the words enter into his heart. Each time a word enters his heart, his chest glows and spark-like embers fall on the floor. When the last word enters into his heart, his eyes glow goldenly then return back to normal. Asoya raises his hands towards the ceiling and worships the God of heaven.

CHAPTER 62

SELF-CONTROL

AFTER SPEAKING IN TWO VILLAGES, ASOYA GRABS A few weighty stones, two pieces of cloth and wraps the stones around his ankles. He then grabs a large stone with a thick piece of rope and ties it to the bottom of both feet. He sighs, rolls backwards, then pulls himself up into a handstand position and starts to do handstand pushups slowly and carefully as he balances the large rock upon his feet.

"I lost my composure in front of Elisa, in front of everyone," he sighs. He stops doing pushups and holds himself up, still balancing the rocks on top of his feet.

"It says in Proverbs 16:32 and Galatians 5:22-23 that he that is able to control his own spirit is mightier than he who is able to take a city. For a ninja, lying waste to a city and leaving it raided is considered an honor; that person is called mighty. But that is not so in the Kingdom of God, for in His Kingdom, the person that has self-control over his/her own spirit is considered mighty. Self-control 自我管理 is one of the fruits of the Spirit, and a teaching that those who are in the light practice."

He ruminates on how to display self-control.

"Lord, forgive me for acting that way in front of everyone," he says as he remembers his actions and the look in Elisa's eyes. He continues to do his pushups and for the remainder of the evening, he practices combative training. *Self-control*, he thinks to himself as he trains in the dark.

CHAPTER 63

TRANG SCOUTS OUT THE LAND

TRANG SCOUTS THE LAND THOROUGHLY TO MAKE SURE no pedestrians or ninjas from other clans are in the surrounding areas. He gathers firewood to create a diversion in case someone decided to slither in on him. As Trang put the firewood in place for the campfire, he drops the last piece of wood, pauses, looks up, and then says, "One who is well learned in the ways of the Koroshiya is here…a *ninja*. Vermillion," as he looks straight ahead sensing Asoya's presence.

Asoya is in a shadow. After a moment, Asoya sits down in it. He sits in the posture that's called Seiza. With back straight, and on his knees; his bottom rests on his ankles as his fists are planted on his outer thighs. He sets his sheathed sword in front of himself on the ground, and closes his eyes.

"Do you remember when we were younger, how much fun we had?" Trang asks with his back facing Asoya.

Asoya grins remembering his childhood in the clan.

"You, Shatter, Pendulum, and I…out of us four, we would joke about who was going to be more like Crimson Wrath 真紅." Trang says reaching for a gold-plated star; he balances the star on one finger.

Crimson? The Adversary of *my new Master…as well as everyone who is born in the flesh*, Asoya thinks knowing that Crimson Wrath is not a ninja, but is *the devil* himself.

"We pillaged cities and villages, but Crimson… Crimson weakens nations! He is the Scarlet dragon 緋色のドラゴン; there is no ninja more violent then him. Crimson Wrath, the first of our kind." Trang says looking at his gold-plated star balancing on his finger.

"Do you remember?" Trang asks chuckling. "Our debates. Which of us four was more like the Scarlet dragon?" Trang's laughter is replaced with resolve. "It was a close one, between you and Pendulum, but even Pendulum knew it was going to be you!"

Trang shouts, turning to the shadow Asoya is sitting in, heaving the gold-plated star at it. The star cuts Asoya's cheek, and continues to spin until it hits a large stone. The stone cracks, shaking the trees around it. Asoya does not move, does not make a sound, he sits with his eyes closed as blood trickles down his face. Trang sighs; turning his back to the shadow Asoya is in. Asoya opens his eyes, rising to his feet slowly; grabbing his sheathed sword.

CHAPTER 64

URAGIRI, BETRAYAL 裏切り

ASOYA STEPS OUT OF THE SHADOWS SLOWLY, SOUND-lessly, just a couple of feet behind Trang.

"I didn't come here to fight with you, Red Velvet."

Trang does not turn to face Asoya, but speaks to him with his back turned, never leaving the spot he was in.

"You've crossed paths with me at a good time, I'm in no mood for battle right now. What do you want?" he asks with a serious tone.

"I am no longer the Vermillion that you once knew," Asoya says quietly.

"Your desertion made that statement quite clear," Trang says.

Asoya sighs then says, "Many of my nerves were damaged from the battles I was involved in. I was in constant pain, but as ninjas, we are taught that pain is weakness, so I bore it. But Jesus healed me of it, and now I feel pain no more."

As Asoya says this he smiles, looking up into the night sky breathing in the cool air.

"Jesus? Who is this Jesus you keep speaking about?"

"I heard about Jesus through a man who was called the Word Carrier. This is the same man whose Master sent me and twelve other men after to assassinate, but we were prevented by a being who would not allow us to eliminate him."

A being? Trang asks himself and turning his head lightly in Asoya's direction as he listens.

"We gain knowledge by observing our enemies. We unravel the schemes of our foes, those who oppose us, but this man was filled with nothing but the love of God 神の愛. I could find no fault in him. I began to listen to the Word Carrier, and he told me about Jesus who is the *Messiah*, The Messiah 救世主 came into the world to save all people from their sins, even those of us who are Japanese. He's done this because we are born into sin. Sin is what separates us from the Omnipotent One, God. So that we would no longer be separated, Jesus had to come here. The Messiah named Jesus is my Master now."

Asoya pauses, then says both sternly and softly, "The Word Carrier also spoke to me about being in the light and in the light, I shall remain 残る. I'm not going anywhere!"

"Not going anywhere," Trang says taking out a gold-plated star. He throws it, and it smashes into a tree that was just a few feet in front of him, shaking loose and dislodging the broken, brittle branches. The branches fall from the tree. Trang breathes heavily as he grabs another star. He was about to throw it at that same tree but stops. He relaxes his breathing as he looks at the star and after a moment of silence, Trang speaks.

"I heard of your fame while I was in the Northern region, the fame of Asoya titled Vermillion the Ruthless One, and your ranking as a Ninja. Master awarded you a sword with the words 'dragon smoke' engraved in the metal, the only sword of its kind. Ruthless Vermillion was the assassin who even caused the clan's ninjas to tremble and quake with terror. You could imagine my joy hearing my friend's stature in the clan. But then I heard of your *uragiri*...betrayal 裏切り."

Uragiri 裏切り, Asoya repeats internally as he listens to Trang. Asoya looks up, seeing that Trang is gripping his gold-plated star tighter then he was previously. Trang speaks on,

"I had to leave the Northern region and return to the Southern quadrant to see for myself. Surely Vermillion would NEVER forsake his creed or commit uragiri. I was willing to crush the ones who spread such lies. I vouched for you, but when I returned, you were nowhere to be seen. I found the rumors to be true. You used everything I taught you against our own clan, against our Master! So, you could understand if I am a bit indignant. How could you betray us? How could you betray me?"

Asoya looks down as he feels the shame of disappointing his old friend. He then looks at Trang and says, "My scuffle is not with you. My intention was not to anger an old friend."

"Intentions … intentions? To turn against the clan is to turn against me, for I am the reason that you entered the arena of being called ninja!"

Asoya pauses, looks up then says, "I'm not leaving this path which I'm currently on. I have been forgiven for the many things that I have done when I was in the shadows by the one that I serve. The Omnipotent One, he's offering you this same forgiveness. He will forgive you; all you have to do is ask and he will forgive you, brother, and cleanse you from your sins that only we who are named Koroshiya understand."

Trang thinks for a moment, really thinks. Deep down forgiveness is something he desires, and in that moment above all else, he wanted forgiveness for the things he committed as a shadow. As he balances the gold-plated star on his finger, Trang spins it, saying, "There is no forgiveness for men like us."

"Hrrmph, there is a God up in heaven that forgives what men like us have done."

There is a long silence … and with that said, Asoya steps into the shadows and disappears.

"Asoya…" Trang says under his breath in anger.

When Asoya returns to his hiding place, he unsheathes his blade and runs his finger against the cold steel. "Red Velvet …" Asoya speaks. He then sews the cut on his cheek shut, placing healing ointment on it.

CHAPTER 65

THE UNFORESEEN MISSION/ASSIGNMENT

ASOYA DID NOT LEAVE HIS PLACE OF DWELLING DURING the day for three weeks. The cut on his face is completely healed; there is no scar. He avoids the orphanage to keep them safe but would travel at night to see if there was clan activity or mention of any activity in the surrounding villages or areas; fortunately, there was not. At home, he read the scrolls and spent his time training.

"It's been three and a half weeks, and Trang has not shown himself. Why even bother? Jesus said not to worry きがかり; I'll just seek the Almighty on where He wants me to go from here," Asoya says to himself. He prays and as he prays, the Lord begins to describe to him the type of person He wants Asoya to bring His word to.

"What? Are you sure, Master?"

When the Lord reconfirms in Asoya's spirit who He wants him to speak to, Asoya says, "Alright, it shall be as you have spoken,

204

Master, it will be done. If you can save somebody like me, then surely you can save this person who you are describing."

He leaves immediately, journeying to the city he was led to. He sees the person he was supposed to speak with amongst the crowd of people. It was a woman, and she stood out from the crowd. Her perfume could be smelled from where Asoya was standing.

"Her perfume can be smelled from here; she is definitely not trying to hide herself at all," he says as he sees the woman enticing men to be with her for the afternoon and a night. She wore a bright red Kimono dress. Asoya shakes his head and sighs. He then says, "Alright, Lord."

He starts to walk in the woman's direction. He lets her know immediately what his purpose is.

"I came to take nothing from you, only to give something to you, and it is life."

"I have a life," she says with a frown. She then smiles and looks at the men who are walking in her direction.

"Do you?" he asks, looking over at the men.

"Look at me," she says, attempting to entice him. Asoya was not moved by the woman's beauty, only by the Word he was carrying. "This way of living was not meant for any woman to live," Asoya asserts.

She wears light makeup; she does not need to wear as much as the traditional Geisha do, for her natural beauty can be seen through the little makeup she wears.

"What is your name?" Asoya asks.

"I am *Geisha* 芸者."

She replies with a smile. "I am Geisha," she repeats. Geisha are a type of prostitute, but unlike regular prostitutes, Geisha are famous for their arts. Some sing, others dance, and others play a string instrument. They entertain their guest by serving them drinks, meals, even a song or traditional dance. Their profession is their art, the Geisha.

"That is not your name" says Asoya and then asks the woman if she would mind if he reads a few passages to her from the book of Proverbs. She nods her head. Asoya begins to read from Proverbs chapter thirty-one. He starts at verse ten and goes all the way down to verse thirty-one. As he reads, he begins to speak to her about a virtuous woman. She listens, almost leaning in, taking in every word.

At first, she thought he was sent there to mock her, until he stops reading and speaks plainly. Asoya tells her that this is who she is, and this is who she was made to be, and this is what she can become, a Proverbs 31 woman. No one has ever spoken to her in this way before. She was used to being told what she was not and what she could not do.

"You were made and created to be a virtuous woman, a woman of honor. All women are."

"How can I be a virtuous woman when I have done all these things? Look at me…" she says as she turns her head to the side in shame. "I am a Geisha."

The woman's words sound all too familiar to Asoya, for in hearing her, he sees himself struggling. Struggling to move forwards knowing that you have a past.

"A past…" he says to himself.

For when she said, "Look at me, I am a Geisha," he heard himself asking in times past, how could I be a Word Carrier, when I was once an assassin?

"There is a God up in heaven who forgives what even a woman, who is known by the name of Geisha has done."

He then starts to show her in God's word different women who were similar to Geisha. He told her about what great Love the Lord has for her and she listens.

"What is your name?" Asoya asks a second time.

She replies, "I am Geisha, no, I mean that I am Katsumi."

"You are Geisha no longer, but rather, you are Katsumi."

Katsumi means 'Victorious Beauty.' She looks down at the ground smiling faintly.

He reaches to his side and grabs ahold of a bag "This in my hand is a bag of money; it's enough yen to hold you over for three years."

Asoya extends his hand and places the bag of money into her hands. She looks down at the bag and tears fill her eyes. "Why are you doing this for me?" she asks as tears roll down her face.

"Because I believe in you, and so does the Lord."

Asoya hands her a few scrolls. One (John 8:1–11) was about the woman who was caught in adultery and the Lord forgave her. The other (Luke 7:36–50) was about the woman who washed Jesus feet with her hair. The other was about a woman in Proverbs 31 and the last (John 4:1–42) was the woman at the well.

"Read these when you start to feel discouraged, meditate on them to remind yourself of how much Jesus really does love you, and how he has come to give you life, and that life truly is found in Him. This should remind you of the woman you were made and created to be. These women were in similar situations as yourself but the Lord forgave them."

"But what if someone recognizes me from my past?"

Asoya looks down and thinks for a moment and then places his eyes back on Katsumi and says, "Then you tell them that you are not that person anymore. You are not the same woman you once were because the Messiah has changed your heart and made you a new creature. Katsumi, the Omnipotent One, the Lord God Almighty has made you new, and he has done this through His Son, Jesus the Messiah."

As Asoya spoke to the woman, he begins to heal from his past. Through what he was saying to Katsumi, he was reminding himself that he, too, is no longer the same Asoya from the clan, but is now a Word Carrier.

CHAPTER 66

SPIES 秘密エージェント

ASOYA LEAVES KATSUMI'S PRESENCE PEACEFULLY AND heads to a stand where a man is selling Daifuku Mochi, also called Habutai Mochi, a type of dessert consisting of a soft rice cake filled with Anko, a sweet red bean. It has been years since he's had it. As he walks, he thinks on being a Word Carrier and realizes how important his assignment was that involved the woman he just spoke with, Katsumi. *This Word really is for everyone and is needed in this land. It must be carried to the people*, he thinks as he walks to the stand. He has a faint smile on his face as he stops walking and looks down at the ground. His smile leaves his face.

"*Spies…*" Asoya says under his breath as he senses the presence of ninjas in the area. Asoya runs outside the town to meet them. He reaches his hand behind his back to take ahold of his sword and pauses as he realizes that it was not there.

"I must have left it at the orphanage," he said to himself as he places his hand back down to his side leisurely and makes a fist.

Back inside the town, Katsumi, who was once called Geisha, stands amazed that someone believes in her and actually gave her something without wanting something in return because of her beauty. Tears roll down her face again. A man walks up to her and asks, "Do you wanna have a good time?"

She looks up slowly. "I'll pay you extra," the man says, thinking that would reel her in.

She looks up at him and says, "My name is Katsumi, and I am a virtuous women. No, thank you. I am no longer a Geisha."

She smiles and then bows. She rises quickly and takes off in the other direction, griping the moneybag and scrolls tightly on her bosom.

"I am accepted in the beloved. Jesus actually loves me and accepts me in His kingdom."

CHAPTER 67

THE PARALYZING INCURSION

" I CAN HEAR THE TAUNTING'S OF YOUR *WHISPERS*...
they do not scare me. Are the shadows your only refuge? The
light is much more fitting, show yourselves," Asoya says to ninjas,
calling them out so that he can drop them all.

Two ninjas harpoon at Asoya from the shadows with blades in
hand. Asoya's dagger was used as a shield as he deflects their multiple blade thrusts. It was as though they are starved sea hunters
from the way they heave their swords at him. He swings his arm
one time, hammering both ninjas on their jaws with his fist; they
were unconscious before they even made contact with the ground.
While they yet fell, a third ninja creeps behind Asoya. Being clandestine, this ninja digs both of his ring fingers into Asoya's lower
back, aggravating a nerve and pressure point. Asoya tumbles to his
knees, losing the use of his legs. This type of move causes temporary paralysis 麻痺.

With haste, Asoya reaches behind his lower back and forces his thumb on the area he was struck, and he twists his thumb with force, causing the pressure point to be released. Asoya now has the use of his legs. His paralysis has ceased. Asoya sprains the ninjas ankle, and bruises the ninja's elbows; this was necessary to stop the assassin from using any of his hidden weapons against Asoya.

"You are the second person to have ever sneak up on me like that. That was clandestine. The first was a young boy."

The ninja, still recovering from the blow he received from Asoya, speaks. "Just because you were the clan's highest-ranking hitman does not mean we fear you."

"Fear?" Asoya asks as he pulls the ninja closer to his face with one hand and points towards the sky.

"Fear? You have no idea the true meaning of the word…fear. It is not me who you should be afraid of but the One I serve. Jesus said fear not those who kill the body, and afterwards have nothing more they can do. Jesus said fear Him who has the power to cast both soul and body in hell," The ninja says nothing, only looks up at Asoya's finger and then upward towards the sky.

"See, my friend, it is not I who you should be worried about. Now you understand what real fear is," Asoya says as he gently taps the ninja on the side of his face. "It's Kingdom stuff, you might want to read this." Asoya places a scroll on the ninja's chest. "And it is for your best interest and benefit that you believe it."

"You are not worthy of the sword that Master awarded you," says the ninja, the ninja continues, "You're a disgrace to those who uphold their creeds, not worthy of being mentioned in the same sentence as the dragon! The shadows, the ninjas, to us you are but smoke."

"Creeds and Ninjas? I'm a Word Carrier."

CHAPTER 68

THE DOOR KNOCK

AT THE NOZAMI ORPHANAGE, ELISA IS TEACHING THE children and the other women that work there about Psalms 91. She is teaching them to memorize it and say it like a prayer; they are reciting it out loud. As they pray, there is a knock on the door. Gēto walks up to the door and slides it open slowly. He looks up and sees a ninja standing at the door.

"Wow…" he says with a smile. "A ninja."

The ninja demands, "Where is Ruthless Vermilion?"

"Huh?" Gēto asks, not understanding what the ninja was asking him.

"I said, where is Vermillion?"

"Vermillion? There's nobody here by that name."

The ninja looks over and sees a sheathed sword propped up against the wall beside the door.

"Then, what is his sword doing over there?" he asks pointing at the sword propped up against the wall. Though it is sheathed, those in the shadows, the ninjas, can recognize this particular sword and its design.

"Oh, that? That belongs to my Master, Asoya."

Elisa rushes to the door upon seeing the shadow agent with a sword behind his back. She grabs Gēto and then gets down on her knees, holding him close to her when she asks, "What do you want?!"

"What do I want?" the ninja asks, taking his eyes off the sword that was against the wall, and looks down at Elisa. The ninja unsheathes his sword that was behind his back then says, "The deserter 脱走兵."

CHAPTER 69

THE LAUGHING SPY

ASOYA TURNS AND STARTS TO WALK AWAY FROM THE ninja, but the ninja laughs.

"Ha, ha, ha…" the spy chuckles.

"You have been incapacitated and are laid out upon the ground, yet you laugh…what's so funny? And do not tell me it is due to gas from a curry bun you ate earlier." Asoya says as he stops walking and looks down at the injured assassin.

"We are the unpredictable. Our philosophy is calibration. When you think there is no strike, one comes. If only you had stayed with us and not strayed. Now, because of you, they have been taken."

Asoya pauses, thinking on the ninja's words, *it can't be,* Asoya thinks as he rushes towards the ninja, grabbing ahold of his shirt with both hands and lifting him into the air. The ninja's feet dangle as he continues to laugh.

"What did you just say, the calibrations, the unpredictable? What do you mean by this?" Asoya asks in anger as he walks backwards until the ninja's back hits a tree. He raises him even higher. He strikes the ninja in his side, right below the last rib. The ninja says nothting, so he strikes him in the same spot again. The ninja flinches from the pain, then continues to laugh. Asoya drops him, walking over to one of the other ninja lying on the ground and grabs ahold of the ninja's blade, taking it from its sheath. He then walks back over to the laughing spy and was about to strike him with the blade, when BOOM! Asoya's heart flashes red as God's word (Ephesians 4:26) comes out of his heart and flashes before his eyes: "In your anger do not sin."

Asoya stares at the words, drops the sword, looks at the ninja, and then runs off. The ninja's laugh could be heard as Asoya disappears into the forest. The dark gray clouds cover the sun. It looks as though it is going to rain, but the clouds hold back their tears as Asoya runs with haste to the only place he could think of—the orphanage.

"*Trang...*" Asoya says under his breath as he grits his teeth. He begins to increase his speed. His heart pumps faster and beats louder, almost like a drum in his head as he tries not to think of what the ninjas did or might have done to the orphans or to Elisa.

CHAPTER 70

THE ORPHANAGE

ASOYA RUSHES BACK TO THE ORPHANAGE IN HOPES that the ninja's words were false, a mere ruse to detour him. As Asoya arrives at the orphanage, he swings open the doors, hoping to find the children, Elisa and the other workers but instead, what he saw was a room filled with a swarm of ninjas and one captive. He sees a woman tied up on the floor with a thick rope around her mouth. She was crying and squirming, and at first, he thought it was Elisa, but upon seeing her face, he knew immediately who it was.

"Chiasa," Asoya says with hesitancy, ashamed that the clan would treat an elderly woman in such a manner, but he knows that ninjas are unpredictable. She looks over at him, shaking her head no, as though to tell him to forget about her.

He looks at the ninjas, and seeing them, Asoya does not think but reacts, rushing pugnaciously towards them. As Asoya runs, his feet trample hard upon the wood floor, making the sound of not one man running but four.

No matter how many stars they throw or how many times they swing their weapons at him, they could not stop Asoya. He doesn't stop until they all are on the ground, not just on the ground unconscious, but deeply bruised and in agony 苦しみ. He hasn't hit anyone as hard as he hit those ninjas since he was last sent on a mission within the clan, since he was last called a Koroshiya. One of the ninjas crawl, trying to escape out of the door. He was unable to run because his leg was injured. Asoya hears the ninja dragging his body across the floor, trying to escape.

"What did you think was going to happen?" Asoya asks. The ninja stops moving for a moment then continues to crawl. "They sent you to retrieve the past shadow named Vermillion. But instead of retrieving me, you all have experienced the weight of my fangs, and are on the floor squirming like dehydrated seals; trying to get back in the water. Tell me assassin, the location of the ones you have taken," says Asoya with exasperation.

The ninja remains silent, and though he was afraid, he does not break his resolve or oath; he remains speechless.

"Tell me NOW!" Asoya picks up one of the ninja's swords and was about to thrust him through, but his chest flashes red yet again, *BOOM!* Words, written in Hebrew appeared 'לב בדיקת' which translate into the words heart check 'לב בדיקת.' God's word from Exodus 20:13 proceed forth from his heart.

ハートチェック

Heart Check/ *Examination*

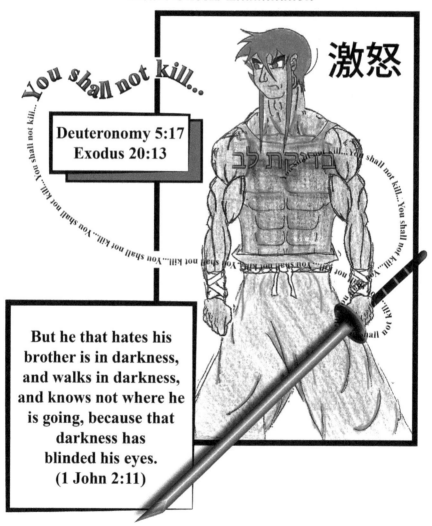

You shall not kill...

Deuteronomy 5:17
Exodus 20:13

激怒

But he that hates his brother is in darkness, and walks in darkness, and knows not where he is going, because that darkness has blinded his eyes. (1 John 2:11)

"Thou shall not kill." So, Asoya falls to his knees and shouts in frustration. He then looks at the sword in his hand, gripping it tighter, but then he eventually drops the sword.

Asoya gets up off his knees and walks over to the ninja, who is still crawling, trying to reach the door. He reaches down and grips the ninja so hard on his trapezius muscle that it affects the ninja's musculocutaneous nerve 筋皮神経 on his right side. Asoya then digs two of his fingers in the ninja's stylohyoid ligament located on the neck on his right side below the jawline and ear, hitting the great auricular nerve 大耳介神経, an internal jugular vein causing the ninja to feel light-headed. Asoya applies just a slight bit more pressure.

"Vermillion has returned," the ninja says, finally speaking and then passes out.

Asoya rushes over to Chiasa. "Are you hurt?" he asks as he quickly unties her and gently loosens the thick rope that is tied around her mouth.

"Are you hurt, Chiasa?" he asks again, repeating the question as he kneels, helping her to her feet. She was hysterical and looks around very shaken.

Asoya puts his hand on her shoulder lightly without any pressure. "It is okay. You are safe now."

Chiasa looks up at Asoya, then around at all the fallen ninja that once held her captive.

"I have never seen anyone move like that, not the way that you just did. How did you defeat all of them? There were so many."

Chiasa pauses as her eyes grow wider, and tears begin to manifest.

"You ... you were once one of them, weren't you?" she asks, looking up at Asoya and backing up slowly.

"Koroshiya ヒットマン," she says, slowly falling to her knees and starting to cry hard.

Asoya looks away, then down at his fist. He frowns, and after giving her a moment, he asks, "Where did they take the children and the workers?"

Chiasa calms down and points in the direction that the ninja's hauled everyone off in. Asoya was about to leave, but she quickly crawls over to where he stood and grabs ahold of his ankle. She looks up, "Please do not become one of them. Even though you were once one of them, you are not them. Don't go back to the shadows, Asoya, but abide under the shadow of the Lord."

"Shadows ..." Asoya says as he sees his sheathed blade propped up against the wall, he grabs it as he runs out the back door with haste.

CHAPTER 71

THE RED VELVET SHURIKEN

ASOYA RAN FOR MILES; MANY LEAVES FALL AS HE gushes past the trees trying to find a trail. He sees Trang out of the corner of his eye a few yards away. Asoya stops himself, but as he stops, his feet slide upon the ground due to the dampness of the leaves, and in so doing, slides past four trees. Once he catches his balance, he turns around and yells, "Trang!"

"What did I tell you about uttering that name? Cease from using it. I thought that you would have been here an hour ago. Tell me, traitor, what took you so long?" Trang asks as he turns to the side and looks down at the ground waiting.

"Where have you taken them?"

"I had no hand in that," Trang says smiling, then turns his head in Asoya's direction. "I hold no interest in the lives of children, only in your capture 捕獲."

"Then who? Who sent them if not you? The clan is involved!"

223

"Master sent three hundred soldiers plus some extra to bring you in. The clan knows full well who you are and will use any means," says Trang.

"Three hundred soldiers? You forgot to say three hundred and one."

"Three hundred and one, do you speak idiocy? Have you not realized by now that I myself am a regiment, I am the clan's brigade, that is why I alone am standing before you, you weakling. I told you the clan is like a noose, do not struggle, but because you have, it is tightening."

"The women and children have been taken! The children were orphans like we once were. Orphans! You know where they are, Red Velvet, tell me where!"

"If you don't return with me within the hour, then they will be …" Trang doesn't finish his sentence, only leisurely shrugs his shoulders. Asoya strikes the tree that is beside him with his fist, and it falls over, exposing the tree's roots. Trang is then splashed by the dampness that was on the leaves that has just fallen, so he wipes his face.

"Cowards … daring to lay hold on those who have no connection to the ways of the shadow," Asoya says.

Upon seeing Asoya's disappointment and the tree with exposed roots, Trang speaks, "Assume nothing but be ready for anything. We are clandestine."

CHAPTER 72

AN ABANDONED HOUSE

ELISA, THE CHILDREN, AND OTHER ORPHANAGE workers were taken hostage and led to an abandoned house.

"Don't any of you move," a ninja says as he points his sword at the children and the other workers who were all tied up and sitting on the floor. The ninja sheaths his weapon, then walks out the front door, and slides the door behind him, locking it.

Gēto looks around suspiciously, looking from left to right.

"He he he," he laughs softly as he lifts his hands into the air. He unties himself. He then pulls the cloth down that was covering his mouth and unbinds his feet, then immediately runs over to Elisa and takes the cloth that was covering her mouth off. She takes a deep breath, then says with awe and surprise, "Gēto, how did you untie yourself? These ties are sophisticated."

Gēto smiles, then replies, "It's a secret." He then unties her hands and then runs around and unties the other workers.

"Are you angry because they are doing what they've been taught?" Trang asks.

Asoya says nothing, he only stares at Trang as though he wants to plow through him but does not.

Trang sees this and speaks on. "As ninjas, we take advantage of every opportunity to cease our enemy. What did you think was going to transpire when you left? That we would not fall upon you? Welcome to the ways of the violent 暴力的な. Now that we have collapsed upon you by force, you are angry."

"I'm going to say this one last time. Tell me where they are!"

"Ha ha! Oh, really?"

Asoya stares on.

"Stop whimpering like a sickly stray dog, you scrawny absconder! They are not your concern anymore, for you have to bout with me. Let's grapple 喧嘩."

"Ahhh!" Asoya yells in rage as he runs at Trang, who just grins as he readies himself for Asoya's attack.

CHAPTER 73

GĒTO THE HELPER

AT THE ABANDONED HOUSE, THE CHILDREN WERE afraid and began to talk while circling the workers and Elisa. Gēto was over by a window. He looks back at the other children and then continues to peek out of the wood window as he lifts it slowly.

"Shhh, it's alright, it's alright, there's no need to be afraid; the Lord is with us. We have to be quiet," Elisa says to the children. She notices Gēto peeking out of the window. He looks down at the ground outside and sees leaves being carried slowly. He then looks up and counts as many ninjas as he could see from the side window. He counted thirty and then lifts the window even higher and shouts, "My master, Asoya, he's gonna get you. He's going to get all of you!"

Elisa quickly covers Gēto's mouth and pulls him back inside the window. She catches the window before it slams shut, then turns and looks at Gēto.

"Gēto, they believe that we are still tied up. Don't give them a reason to come back in here. This is not a game; the ninjas are serious."

"But Asoya is going to get them. He's gonna save us."

"We can't place our trust in Asoya, Gēto, but the Lord."

"But … but …" Gēto says as he looks into Elisa's eyes. Her eyes water, and he sees the tears. He then sits down and crosses his legs, propping his hand on his chin. "Yeah, okay," he says frowning.

Elisa uses her forearm to wipe her tears, and then bends down and places her hands on Gēto's shoulders.

"I need your help, Gēto. Could you help me with the other children? Help me calm them down. Can you do that?"

He looks up at Elisa, then smiles and says, "Yeah, I can do that, Ms. Elisa. You are like my mother. No, you *are* my mother."

As he gets up, he remembers the words of Asoya. He instructed Gēto to protect the other children and to help Elisa when he can. He takes two steps back, and then bows before Elisa. He rises and runs over to where the other children are.

CHAPTER 74

ASOYA FORAYS

ASOYA DASHES AT TRANG, THROWING HIS RIGHT LEG towards the side of Trang's face. Trang blocks the attack with his left hand. Asoya's foot was eight centimeters from the side of Trang's face. Trang turns and looks at Asoya's wooden sandal.

"You're wearing *geta's*, how fitting." Geta are wooden Japanese sandals.

Trang swiftly turns his wrist and grabs hold of Asoya's ankle. He balls up his fist and attempts to bruise the left side of Asoya's abdomen. Asoya blocks it with the back of his left forearm. Trang sweeps Asoya's other leg from under him; Asoya reaches his right hand behind his head and catches himself before hitting the ground. He then kicks Trang with his left leg, hitting Trang in the stomach. Trang slides backwards, then looks up smiling.

Asoya rushes towards Trang, giving him his elbow, which nearly reaches Trang's neck. Trang catches Asoya's elbow with his palm, then pushes Asoya back. Asoya takes the two fingers on his right hand and strikes Trang on his side, hitting a pressure point. Trang grabs Asoya's two fingers, then strikes Asoya on the torso with an open palm. Asoya skids backwards, then grabs his chest, looking up at Trang. Asoya frowns.

"That attack could have stopped my heart immediately. He's not just targeting nerves on the body as I do…but internal muscles, and organs 臓器." Asoya states quietly as he pats his chest feeling that his heart was still beating.

Trang was looking down with his palm still extended in Asoya's direction. He closes his palm, making a fist, looks up at Asoya, and then frowns as well. A cool breeze brushes through the tops of the trees. The leaves from the surrounding trees make their way to the ground, twirling slowly. A leaf lands softly in front of Asoya. He extracts his blade from its sheath. Trang does the same with pleasure.

絶望

Despair

の芸術
消耗

Koroshiya / Hitman use
the shadows...
the shadow is always
ready.

CHAPTER 75

THE PRAYING CHILDREN

AT THE ABANDONED HOUSE, THE CHILDREN PRAY.

"Lord, please protect Mr. Asoya … and …um …" Smiles says as she looks around at everyone smiling. She then closes her eyes and says, "Help me be nicer."

The boy sitting next to her opens his eyes and looks at her. "But you're already nice."

"I know," she says with a smile. "I just want to be even nicer."

Elisa smiles. "Did you want to pray?" Elisa asks a shy boy who was seated next to her.

"Yes…" he says shyly.

"It's okay, go ahead," Elisa encourages him.

He closes his eyes and says, "Dear Lord Jesus, please give us all *Momiji Manju* because they are really good."

All the children laugh. Momiji Manju is a castella cake that is filled with sweet red bean paste and is shaped like an autumn leaf, thus the name Momiji.

"Momiji? Why would you pray for the autumn leaf cake?" a girl asks.

"Because they're good!" he says with a frown. The children continue to laugh. He softens up his face and laughs too.

The Lord tries to get Asoya's attention, but he was so focused on his battle with Trang that he did not hear Him.

CHAPTER 76

BLADES

TRANG JOLTS AT ASOYA, BLADE FIRST, AND HIS MOVE-ment was like a shark about to make a kill shot as it bullets through the water with speed. Asoya's blade catches Trang's. The blades claw and scrape across one another as they clash. Asoya sees an opening to attack, so he elbows Trang on his shoulder where the scar is located, causing Trang's arm to tingle. Asoya spins, then swings his blade at Trang's thighs, and Trang jumps up, then lands on the flat part of Asoya's sword. Asoya fist plows into Trang's *tibia* 脛骨, this bone is located between his kneecap and ankle.

Stunned, Trang backs up, but before he was able to swing his blade, Asoya rises, uppercutting the base of Trang's jaw, then spin kicks him. Trang flies back, crashing through a tree. He stops as his back hits the bark of a second tree, and he hits the ground. After squeezing a few leaves, Trang rises slowly, wiping the blood from his mouth with the leaves. He then rubs his shoulder around the scar, smiles, and says, "*This* is the ninja I remember."

"Ahhh!" Asoya yells as he hurdles at Trang like a manic shark, fist-first.

Trang clasps Asoya's fist in his hand. "He, he…" Trang jests mockingly as he looks at Asoya's fist.

Asoya unleashes an onslaught of calculated attacks, and Trang counters, blocking them all. There were several times where Trang could have issued damaging blows to Asoya, but he does not. Each time he refrains from using an attack that could leave Asoya crippled, Trang's core tugs at him. He is ninja, and ninjas deliver blows that will cripple or permanently put down their targets. These are the rules that the clan has set in place for every assassin to follow. Deep down, he really has no desire to battle with Asoya, but although Red Velvet did not want to fight, he was finding enjoyment in his battle with Asoya.

Trang attempts to hit Asoya in the kidney, but Asoya stops the strike with his shin then aims to bury his fist into Trang's face. Trang chuckles as he ducks, and as he ducks, Asoya's fist embeds itself in the bark of the tree. The bark bursts around his fist as the tree rumbles, causing more leaves to be shaken. They break off the branches and drift around him like a showering mist.

While Asoya's fist was caught in the tree, Trang uses this time as an opportunity to assault. He issues a strategized blitz 砲撃. He lairs two of his knuckles in Asoya's inner leg, then the side of his kneecap; Asoya loses temporary function in his legs and falls. As Asoya was falling backwards, Trang knees him in the chest. Air was knocked out of Asoya's right lung, and he hits the ground, sliding backwards in the mud and slushy leaves. Asoya pushes himself back up with one hand as though nothing happened, brings the hilt of his blade close to his face, then extends his free hand in Trang's direction, glaring.

"Look at you standing after I issued you a cuardenated blitz. You're the only one I know who can do so. You were made for this." Trang states as he watches Asoya attack stance.

Asoya's attack stance was flawless. His blade moves gradually as he studies his attacker before him, Red Velvet. Asoya was stagnant, searching for an opening, and as he searches, he remains well postured. His attitude in that moment was that of a ready ninja.

CHAPTER 77

THE PSALM 91 PRAYER

"REMEMBER HOW WE MEMORIZED PSALM 91:1 AND have been praying it for several weeks? Let's pray it out loud together right now," Elisa says as they were all seated. Everyone closes their eyes and starts to pray, but Gēto raises his hands towards the ceiling, looking up as he prays.

"He who dwells in the secret place of the Most High shall abide under the shadow of the Almighty."

***

Noticing the way that Asoya is postured, Trang knows that he is doing calculations, so he grins. "The shadows, they are calling to you beckoning you, to embrace you," he says as he changes the hand that he was holding his sword in.

"You are mistaken, they are not calling to me. The light is my domain," Asoya says in response.

Trang sighs then says, "We were your refuge, a fortress from being disregarded as an orphan. Your blade was your trust. Who will deliver you now from the hands of the clan?"

***

"He is our refuge and fortress our God, in him will I trust. Surly he shall deliver thee," Elisa and the children said Psalm 91:2 as they all raise their hands towards the ceiling, giving reverence to the Almighty One.

***

"Still calculating? Come now, I've taught you better than this; have you forgotten your training already?" Trang asks Asoya.

"I don't have time to play your games, tell me where they are!" Asoya asks forcefully, impatient to find the workers and the children's location.

"Make me," Trang says as he signals to Asoya to come after him, taunting him. Asoya swipes his sword at Trang. He swings so hard that it shakes the leaves in the trees and causes a few leaves to rise off the ground. Trang moves to the side, sheaths his own sword, then grabs Asoya by the wrist with his left hand and chops him on the shoulder blade with his right hand. POP! ポップ When Trang's hand meets Asoya's shoulder, he pops Asoya's arm out of its socket.

"Arghhh!" Asoya hollers in pain. He quickly does a spin kick, kicking Trang to put some distance between them. Trang is hit between his abdomen and ribs and zooms backwards. Asoya quickly grabs his dislocated arm by the shoulder, but before he could gain enough composure to put it back in its place, Trang retaliates violently, propelling darts one right after the other. Asoya does two backflips with one hand. Another dart flies by him; then he does another backflip with no hands and lands three inches from a tree.

He precipitously does a cartwheel with no hands, but right when Asoya flips, two darts land into the bark of the tree with a loud thud ドキドキ音. Asoya dodges the darts as best as he can, but Red Velvet was able to make one land in Asoya's leg. Asoya yanks it out, then falls to one knee, holding his shoulder due to the discomfort. Trang reaches behind his back and extracts his sword.

***

"Surely, he shall deliver thee from the snare of the fowler..." everyone inside of the house says as they pray to the Almighty, taking shelter in Him.

Blood flows from Asoya's leg where the dart once was; he looks down at it, still holding his dislocated arm. He slowly looks over at Trang. "He's trying to ensnare me just like a flowler does a bird. I've got to create a diversion to get around Trang to get to everyone," Asoya says to himself.

"Stalling, are we? Attempting to figure out an approach to get around me? I know how you think. Remember, I taught you everything you know. I know what you are thinking before you even think it," says Trang

"Not everything," Asoya replies as he throws a smoke bomb at a tree that was close to him. It combusts, causing red smoke to quickly cover the area like a storm cloud.

"Red smoke? That's a Hatsuentou Bomb 発煙筒! Where did he get that?" Trang asks as he sees the thick red smoke overtake the area. He looks down at his side and reaches into his side pouch; he was missing two bombs because Asoya relieved him of them. Two stars flutter out of the smoke in Trang's direction. Trang's sword claws at the first star and then repels the other. Asoya uses the second smoke bomb and casts it out of the smoke. When it was halfway in front of Trang, Asoya threw a rock at the bomb. It fizzes before erupting, BOOM 景気拡大! Smoke rushes through the area around Trang, and his hearing is temporarily impaired from it erupting to close too his face.

Asoya runs and bounces off a tree and kicks, pointing his foot at Trang. Trang sees him coming in his direction from his peripheral vision, but it's too late. Asoya's foot makes contact with his back. Trang is sent forward and smashes through two trees. He finally stops soaring by landing in a bush. Asoya uses that time to run and find the ones who were captured.

"Asoya…" Trang says as he pushes the tree off himself. He then rises sluggishly out of the bush, picks up his blade, and chases after Asoya.

CHAPTER 78

HIDE AND SEEK かくれんぼ

ELISA PRAYS AS THE CHILDREN STILL HAVE THEIR ARMS extended towards the ceiling. Gēto's eyes remain open as he watches everyone, but after a few seconds, he closes his eyes.

"I thank you, Lord, that you will deliver us from this snare that the ninjas have set up for us and from those who have spread out a net under our feet to trap us and try to entangle us," says Elisa.

***

Asoya continues to run, maneuvering in and out of the trees, spotting the tracks that the ninjas took upon taking everyone at the orphanage. His chest flashes red a third time. BOOM! He grabs his chest, seeing these words from Psalm 46:10: "Be still and know that I am God. I will be exalted among the heathen. I will be exalted in the earth."

"Be still? Be still? How can I be still when everyone at the orphanage have been taken? They only left behind Chiasa. I have to find them," says Asoya as he rushes between two trees and past some bushes. He grunts as he grabs ahold of his arm and urgently pops his dislocated shoulder back in place.

God's word continues to flash before his eyes.

"And besides, how can I to be still when Trang is on my tail, making combat with me? He does not want a truce, but a battle." Still running, he stretches his arm.

He sees more words, this time from 2 Chronicles 20:15: "The battle is not yours but it is the Lord's."

"The battle is not mine, but it is yours, Lord?" ask Asoya as he hears Trang's footsteps treading upon the leaves in the distance.

"A game of hide and seek! So, you want to sport by running? You make hunting so rousing, he he haaa! " Trang shouts, sprinting amidst the trees.

Asoya stops and rips a part of his shirt and ties it around his leg tightly to stop the bleeding. He tries to keep some distance between them at this time due to him being injured. He hides behind a tree; when he hears where Trang's location is, he commences casting stars in that direction. Trang hears them coming so he deters four stars, then ducks behind a tree.

Asoya breathes hard then tries to run, but Trang's attacks of spinning stars thwarted his efforts. Asoya bashes three of them out of the air with a swing of his blade then gets behind a tree.

"Enough!" Trang yells as he slices the tree he was hiding behind in two and then kicks it in Asoya's direction. Asoya hears branches crashing, so he turns around to see a tree coming his direction. He jumps, slices the tree, then hides behind another tree.

***

Inside the abandoned house, they continue speaking in unison, reciting Psalm 91:3.

"Surely he shall deliver thee from the snare of the fowler and from the noisome pestilence."

As they pray, the ninjas start to gather together because time was running out. It has almost been an hour since Asoya and Trang have been competing. The ninjas make a half-circle around the house where Elisa and the children were being held captive. The ninjas are just a few yards away, but the children pray on, continuing onto Psalm 91:4: "He shall cover thee with his feathers"

A few of the ninja's start digging a hole in the ground. When they make a small hole, they throw wood down into it.

"...and under his wings shalt thou trust."

The ninjas that dug the hole took ointment from there pouches and pour it on the wood, then strike two rocks together making a spark and the wood catches fire.

Elisa takes over praying. "Lord, in You do we trust, WE TRUST, we trust under Your wings, under Your protection."

The ninjas, who dug the hole, got back in line as the ninjas with bows stand in front of the fire. They take a cloth and wrap it around the arrow, then place their arrows on their bows. They put the part of the arrow with the cloth around it in the fire, and the arrow ignites. The children and workers join Elisa in praying as they speak verse four of Psalms 91.

".... his truth shall be thy shield and buckler."

***

"Where are you? Since when have you started allowing bark to be your buckler? Stop using the trees as a shield, return to us and let us be your cover again. I know you're tired of running. The orphans were taken because of your cowardice," Trang says, growing weary of pursuing Asoya.

Asoya thinks about the orphans as he takes out his dagger, rising slowly. A tree collapses and Trang turns only to see Asoya standing where the tree once stood. With a dagger in one hand and his sword in the other, he stares at Trang, saying "Hide and seek is OVER! Now, what will Trang do? Asoya runs from no one."

247

CHAPTER 79

CHIPPED SHURIKENS AND CRACKED METAL

"I'M GLAD THAT YOU'VE STOPPED RUNNING. WHAT would Elisa say if she knew that you ran away from me like a weakling?"

"Elisa," Asoya says, getting out of his attack stance and standing upright. He looks up at the clouds that are now dark and moving like an ocean tide.

"I'm about to give you something that a ninja has never given you before by their own hands," Asoya says, almost in a trance-like state as he drags his dagger across his own blade three times while still watching the clouds. Shard-like embers fall to the ground from sparking due to him dragging the dagger across the metal with such dynamism.

"And what would that be?" Trang asks.

"Pain … 傷つける," Asoya replies. Asoya no longer watches the clouds but gazes at Trang instead. He launches his dagger at

Trang, who lifts his sword to shield himself from the dagger. The dagger rams into his sword, lifting Trang into the air, who then hits the cold leaves and mud and lands on his side and slides until his back hits the tree behind him. Trang quickly grabs his hand to stop the tingling. He rises and shouts, "I am the clan's Brigade 旅団, the Red Velvet Shuriken!" Trang takes out six gold-plated stars, three in each hand. Asoya looks down at his sword that he was holding and gradually moves it from side to side.

"Your name is nothing," Asoya says, engrossed by the sword in his hand. Six stars fly but are all cut down. Asoya does not even glance at them but only moves his weapon, and when he does, the stars hit the ground. It was reflex, an automatic response, an instinct 本能. He then looks at Trang, but the look that he gave him was hollow, empty. Trang has seen this look before; it was the same eyes that he had in the clan years ago when he first became Vermillion. At that moment, Trang knew that he was no longer facing Asoya, but the feared Koroshiya, Vermillion, the clan's gladiator. Vermillion runs towards Trang without the intent of wounding him; he wants to shed Trang's blood 流血.

Trang takes out more shurikens and fires them rapidly as though they were burning his hands, but Vermillion does not stop coming; his pursuit was certain. The stars bend and chip from being thrown so hard, but Vermillion's sword cracks from being swung so brutally as the stars ram against his steel. Trang is reached, and Vermillion burrows three of his fingers in Trang's calf muscle on his left leg without breaking the skin. The veins in his entire leg shift, and the muscles tighten. He then taps Trang twice in the same spot using his thumb. をタップ TAP! TAP! The second tap had more force applied to it then the first, which causes his calf to spasm and cramp. It was like seven hornet stings concentrated in one spot, undoubtedly excruciating. He hits Trang with a second attack. He strikes him on his right leg down by the side of his knee, his knee shifts, making his kneecap pop out of its place.

Trang falls, but before he fully hits the mud, Vermillion grabs hold of his trapezius muscle, the muscle between the neck and shoulder, lifting Trang into the air with one hand. Vermillion squeezes Trang's trapezius tighter, fracturing Trang's collarbone. Trang yells in pain, never having felt such anguish before because he had never experienced the Gladiator head-on, only Asoya, his brother. Trang reaches over with his other hand and tries to pry himself free from the grip of Vermillion, but he could not. Vermillion raises Trang higher into air and bangs his back into the tree that was behind him. Vermillion looks at Trang's face, then points his cracked sword at him.

"Kowagaru," Vermillion says with a raspy voice, and emptiness in his eyes. Kowagaru means to fear, to be afraid of, dread or feel terror. Kowagaru 怖がる. A word spoken by one that is Ruthless 冷酷, the weapon named Vermillion.

251

CHAPTER 80

REALIZATIONS

A SHARK HAS CLAMPED DOWN HIS FANGS, AND TRANG is stuck in the very jaws of this shark. He looks down seeing the hollowness in Vermillion's eyes.

That look…it is the look of Satsujin, Trang thinks as he feels Vermillion's sword touching his shoulder. Satsujin is the philosophy of slaughtering, murder 殺人. This is the look of a ready predator, a hitman ヒットマン.

"I'm glad to have you back, Vermillion, even if it's to my harm. I welcome it if it means you become the weapon that you were made to be," Trang says with pain in his voice from the throbbing on his collarbone, calf muscle and kneecap. Vermilion says nothing, he only looks at different spots on Trang's body; trying to see where his sword would cause the most pain.

"Doesn't it feel good to have your sword be an extension of your savagery once again?"

Vermillion taps Trang's shoulder with his sword.

"Your speaking is gibberish; end it. My blade is the only thing that is going to talk to you now," Vermillion says.

"Whatever you have to do, do it, Vermillion, this is what it means to be a hitman ヒットマン," Trang says, closing his eyes with a satisfied smile, glad that Vermillion has returned.

"It's so good to see you holding something other than a scroll in your hand, brother," Trang says, seeing a newfound resolve in the clan's Gladiator.

"Scrolls?" Vermillion asks, suddenly being aware of what he was holding, just his sword and not a scroll.

"You are holding the only truth that you once knew, your BLADE! How does it feel to have your blade to be your trust once again?"

A leaf drifts down and lands on Asoya's blade, his blade. The Word that he was carrying instantly came into his mind. His name is Asoya and not the clan's Gladiator, Vermillion. He drops Trang. Trang hits the mud while Asoya recalls what is written in Psalm 44:6.

"I will not trust in my bow," Asoya says as he backs away from Trang, sliding his sandals across the leaves. Asoya was looking down at his own sword as he continues to walk backwards. When these words were said about not trusting in his bow, the ninjas drew back their bows, aiming, ready at any moment to release their arrows upon the house where the orphans and Elisa were praying.

253

"Neither shall my sword save me," Asoya says, understanding the verse. It became real to him, a reality 現実; more than just words on a page, more real than the blade he was holding. Trang puts his knee back in its place and sits up, looking at Asoya. He then hits a pressure point on his shoulder and neck area to relieve the pain he was feeling in his collarbone. Asoya pauses, looking at his own arm and the sword that was in his hand. He drops his sword.

***

The children and Elisa are still talking to the Almighty One, speaking His word from Psalm 91:5.

"Thou shalt not be afraid for the terror by night; nor for the arrow that flieth by day."

The ninjas that had their bows bent back release their fire arrows.

"For he shall give his angels charge over thee ..." As soon as those words were spoken by Elisa and the children, there was a bright flash of light in the sky. BANG ばたん! The sound of a cannon's blast could be heard as it flashes. When the light declines, an angel came speeding down from the sky, shield first towards the earth as said in Psalm 91:11: "For he shall give his angels charge over thee, to keep thee in all thy ways."

CHAPTER 81

THE GUARDIAN 天使のような存在

THE FIERY ARROWS ARE HALFWAY TO THE HOUSE BUT

are stopped. Like a meteor that crashes into the earth, the angel crashes into the ground, shield first. The ground shakes as a deep crater is made from the impact of the angel's landing. An explosion of rocks, dirt and grass fly everywhere.

All the flames that the ninjas had lit to ignite their arrows were put out by the force of the angel's impact. All the flaming arrows they shot at the house stopped at the crater and were stopped by the flying debris of rocks and dirt. The ninjas remain motionless as the thick clouds of dirt dissipated.

The angel slowly floats to the top of the crater. As he floats, the ground beneath him starts to repair itself from the damage of his crash landing. The last bit of dirt and grass went back to their place; it was as if the damage to the ground was never done. Then, the angel lands, placing his feet on the repaired ground beneath him.

He takes off his helmet and places it under his arm. He then takes out a glowing sword and impels it into the ground in front of him. The angel looks at the ninjas that are scattered throughout the area and then speaks, "You will step no further."

End of *Asoya*: **Shadows From the Past:**
Trang (忍者、ヒットマン) Section 3

忍者、ヒットマン
Section 4

The Piranha's, the Sharks and the Ploy

ピラニア　　　　鮫　　　　策略

CHAPTER 82

PLOY 権謀

THE MOMENT AN ASSASSIN HAS SOMEONE LOCKED IN his or her sights, a ploy emerges. They strategize on how to get the person in their sights, what has been ordered by the clan, and how it can be accomplished. They do this by planning how to bring down the one they are sent after. A scheme スキーム, has an end in mind, to set in motion a hidden agenda that has been systematically arranged without the person's knowledge, and that scheme is to that individual's ruin. Because Trang saw with his own eyes that Asoya was a 法律違反者 lawbreaker, a ploy was set in motion to get him to return to the shadows from whence he was once shrouded by any means necessary.

CHAPTER 83

THE ONE WHO SAVES US FROM OUR ENEMIES

IT STARTS TO RAIN LIGHTLY, CAUSING MORE LEAVES to soar downwards from the trees.

"For I will not trust in my bow, neither shall my sword save me. But thou (You) hast (have) saved us from our enemies, and hast (have) put them to shame that hated us," Asoya says reciting the words from Psalm 44:6–7 that he was carrying. Asoya realizes what he has done. He collapses to his knees and smashes his fist into the damp mud. He then brings his hand over his face and shakes his head. He grasps that he's been trusting in himself and not in the power of the Almighty 全能. It is the Lord who saves His people from their enemies and not their own hands.

"I'm not going to fight you anymore, Red Velvet, for the battle is not mine, but the Lords."

"What?" he asks, rising to his feet, holding his arm.

"Koroshiya Vermillion, the Ruthless One, that the other ninjas feared was standing before you, that man is not standing before you now." says Asoya. Trang sees that the look of Satsujin, which is the philosophy of slaughtering and murder that he just witnessed in Asoya's eyes, is now gone. Trang kicks the tree behind him three times as rage envelops him from the words Asoya just spoke. His foot imprint is left in the tree as the branches break off and fall.

"Lord, I've been trying to save and rescue the children, the workers and Elisa by my own might, rather than trusting and relying upon Your ability to save them."

"Shut your mouth, shut your mouth, or I will shut it for you!" Trang yells, taking out the last of his shurikens and points them at Asoya.

***

Back at the abandoned house, two other angels came down, drifting slowly and wearing white garments. Their sandals touch the ground gently. They look at each other and then at the third angel wearing the armor. He was pacing the ground, walking back and forth, as though to dare any of the ninjas to try to pass him.

"Wha...what are you?" one ninja asks the angel who is pacing back and forth wearing armor.

The angel responds, saying the words from Psalm 104:4: "A minister of flaming fire, sent forth to protect the heirs of righteousness."

The angel went over to where his sword was and grabs ahold of the handle, pulling it out of the ground. He then disappears and reappears in front of the ninjas.

***

Asoya continues to speak to the Almighty One.

Trang violently heaves the five stars at Asoya.

Asoya's chest flashes red as gold-colored words proceed out of his heart, encircling him, the shurikens crash into the words that read: "the shadow of the Almighty." Asoya is protected, and the shurikens then fall to the ground.

Enraged, Trang runs up to Asoya and performs a spin kick in the air. The back of Trang's heel met Asoya's jaw, so he was lifted off the ground and whirls in the air from the power of Trang's heel. Asoya whirls wildly several times then hits the ground, rolling, tossing and tumbling. He finally stops rolling and lays there unconscious.

"Did not I say you would return with me this day?" Trang says with sadness on his face and in his voice. He sighs deeply, then rises slowly, frowning once more.

"Willingly," Trang says, grabbing ahold of his blade's handle, pulling it out slowly from its sheath. "Or by the edge," he says as he rotates his sword downwards, the sharp end faces Asoya. He tightens his grip and places his other hand on the hilt, holding his blade's handle firmly with both hands.

"Of my BLADE!" Trang shouts as he thrusts his blade downwards on Asoya. As soon as he brings his blade down on Asoya, he has a memory—Trang's memory was from the time when he was seventeen and Asoya was fifteen. Trang was hanging on the edge of a cliff with one hand and was slipping.

"Trang!" Asoya shouted as he made it to the edge of the cliff on the side of a mountain. He slid on his knees, got on his hands, and looked down. He saw Trang hanging by one hand, firmly gripping a stone.

"Leave me. Complete the mission," Trang said as he looked up at Asoya. Asoya breathed heavily, almost in a panic. He looked back toward the mountain top and then back down at Trang.

"But ... Tra..."

"LEAVE!" Trang shouted, closing his eyes tightly as his voice echoed in his own ears.

Asoya left. The rock Trang was holding onto started to loosen and shift.

The present:

He refuses to allow the rest of the memory to play out. He looks at his sword that he thrust down on Asoya; it was right next to Asoya's head. Asoya was unharmed by Trang's blade. He simply could not bring himself to hurt his old friend anymore than he already has, for he still considers Asoya his brother.

He lets out a shout, then breathes forcefully as he looks down at Asoya lying there unconscious. He realizes that Asoya would not leave the path that he was on, the path of light 光. He rises, pulls his blade out of the ground, cleans it; and then places it back within his sheath. He turns to walk off but pauses as the wind blows, carrying with it the autumn leaves. He looks down at his brother one last time and then disappears into the forest.

***

The angel ran through the mist of ninjas swinging his blade; over two hundred ninjas were scattered about in that location, but the angel ran through them all. He sheaths his weapon, turns, and looks at the two hundred ninjas, seeing that their weapons all shatter at the same time like glass.

The angel then stomps his foot on the earth and, lets out a war cry. Energy proceeds from his body and rushes through the mist of the ninjas, rendering the rest of their weaponry to powder as told in Isaiah 37:36. The other two angels, wearing the white garments, float into the air and form a barrier, a hedge of protection around the house that Elisa and the children were in as the other angel fought.

CHAPTER 84

ELISA AND MAKOTO

INSIDE THE ABANDONED HOUSE, EVERYONE IS LOOKING out the windows, watching the angel protect them from the ninjas. They are all amazed and astonished that the Lord sent one of His angels to guard them.

The lady who walks with a limp has a knife hidden behind her back; her name is Makoto.

Elisa turns around and sees Makoto walking towards her slowly and says, "Makoto, are you alright?"

Seeing a serious look on Makoto's face, Elisa asks again, Makoto doesn't respond. She stops walking then slowly takes out the knife.

"Makoto, what are you doing?" she asks, startled.

"Fulfilling my mission." says Makoto

"Mission? What do you mean?" Elisa he asks in a panic.

Makoto looks at the knife and then looks at Elisa before saying, "I can no longer fight alongside my fellow ninjas. Ever since I was wounded in a battle, now I walk with this limp, so they make use of me by sending me in as a spy, doing undercover work."

"Makoto, nooooo," Elisa says, as tears fill her eyes as she remembers the words Asoya spoke concerning her.

The angel looks up into the sky, then closes his eyes, hearing the voice of God. The angel opens his eyes and says, "Yes, Lord." The angel turns towards the house, then flies at it like lightning. It sounded like a cannon went off when he flew toward the house.

"It's nothing personal. A ploy is a ploy; an assassin must do what they have been assigned; these are the oaths we make," Makoto says with a smile.

Elisa closes her eyes as a tear rolls down her cheek.

The angel crashes into the house, bursting through the wall, landing in front of Elisa.

Makoto ran at Elisa to stab her with her knife extended in front of her. Fortunately, her knife met an invisible shield in front of the angel, causing it to bend then snap. Makoto looks at her blade and then at the angel who is glaring at her. She drops the other half of the knife and runs off screaming. Elisa opens her eyes only to see the back of an angel standing in front of her.

The angel turns to look at Elisa. He then flies outside, leaving the same way he came in and just as quickly.

268

Gēto follows the angel by running after him. The angel stops, his feet touch the ground gently. Gēto catches up with him.

The angel turns and looks at Gēto. "You are a guardian, aren't you? Did you train my master, Asoya?" Gēto asks with exuberance.

The angel smiles and then looks up as he sees Elisa running toward them from the house. Elisa falls before the angel with her face towards the ground. She thanks the angel for saving her and starts to worship him.

The angel speaks, reciting Revelation 22:8–9, "DO NOT worship me ... WORSHIP GOD! For He alone is worthy. I am His mere servant, sent forth to protect those who fear Him."

As he speaks, he starts to float, then he shoots off into the air, disappearing into the clouds. There was thunder, a lightning flash, then quietness.

"Cool ..." Gēto says, staring up into the sky with a big smile.

***

A large water droplet collects under a branch on a tree; the droplet releases itself from the branch and hits Asoya on his head. He wakes up in a panic, looking around for Trang, but Trang was gone.

He sheaths his blade, then runs looking for Elisa and the other children. He finds them twenty minutes later, so he stops to catch his breath and sprints over to them. He sees the ninjas lying on the ground motionless. *Did Trang do this?* He wonders. He sees Elisa on her knees with her palms extended upwards towards the sky, glorifying God.

"Master Asoya!" Gēto says as soon as he sees him. Gēto enthusiastically gets Elisa's attention, and she rises, rushing to Asoya.

"The Lord delivered us, Asoya! The Lord delivered us!" she says with tears of joy "He sent His—" Gēto interrupts Elisa.

"Master Asoya, you should have seen the Guardians. Three came, but only one fought. He was like Sha-Boom! Shik-Ka-Boom! HA-KA-POWY! That was the noise his attacks made each time he hit the ninjas."

"The Guardians?" Asoya says, looking at all the ninja lying on the ground.

"They came. The Almighty One sent them to protect those who feared and trusted in His name," Asoya says to himself, reaching down to check one of the ninja's vital signs; he was still breathing faintly with a pulse. Over two hundred of them laid there on the ground, sleeping.

"If only one Guardian did this, imagine what a whole army could have done. No one can make war against the armies of the Living God," he says, looking up towards the sky.

"Lord, your arm is mighty to save. It is not too short but mighty."

References to this story can be found in Psalm 44:3, Isaiah 59:1, Deuteronomy 33:27 and Exodus 6:6.

CHAPTER 85

NEW NOZAMI ORPHANAGE

THE REBUILDING OF THE NEW NOZAMI ORPHANAGE

was under construction. Elisa wanted to stay in the same house the orphanage was already in, but Asoya convinced her to move to a new location. Elisa and a few of the workers go to a nearby village to buy food. As they shop, Elisa begins to tell many people about God's delivering power to those who trust in Him and dwell in Him.

The other workers nod their heads in agreement, bearing witness to the Lord's ability to deliver them. After the orphanage was finished being built, Asoya disappears. *I cannot return to this place*, he thinks, knowing that if the clan tracks and pursues him again, their lives would once again be in danger.

CHAPTER 86

THE CLIFF'S EDGE

IT IS NIGHTTIME. THE RAIN BEGINS TO POUR AS THE skies open, releasing its water. Asoya sits in the dark, thinking as flashes of light from the lighting pierce the darkness in the room. He thinks about how the Lord delivered Elisa and the children. He then ponders about Trang and wonders why he didn't bring him in.

"Was it because of that day?" Asoya asks out loud as he looks up, staring straight ahead at the wall. He was glancing at the painting that Elisa gave him. "That day on the edge of the cliff?"

Lighting strikes again, brightening up the room. As the room returns to darkness, Asoya remembers the mission he went on with Trang where he received most of his scars and where Trang received his. Trang was seventeen, and Asoya was fifteen.

"Assume nothing but be ready. Be ready for anything; do you understand?" Trang asked, instructing Asoya while they hid from a rival clan. They were hiding not because of fear but to formulate a strategy 戦略. Asoya nodded his head slowly up and down to say yes.

"This is our mission, to take out one of our rival clans, the Shin Obi's lookout posts that are at the top of this mountain," Trang said as he turned his head and pointed his finger toward their rival's location.

"The Shin Obi are like Piranha; they are not to be taken lightly, but neither are we. We are Sharks; the shark fears no creature. Even though we are attacking during the day, we must not allow ourselves to be seen; we are clandestine."

Asoya saw the serious look on Trang's face. *Clandestine,* Asoya repeated within himself.

Trang continued to instruct, saying, "Piranhas are dangerous. Once they bite you, they do not stop, but we don't take little baby bites as they do; we clamp down our fangs once, then swallow our enemies whole! What are we like, Asoya?"

"Sharks," Asoya said with a smile.

Trang placed his hand on Asoya's shoulder. "Very good, brother. We own the shadows. We are sharks."

Trang turned and looked at Asoya, who nodded his head at Trang. "Alright, let's go."

Trang signaled to Asoya what part of the mountain to climb. Asoya snuck to the base of the mountain, tied his sword to his back, and then started to climb. Trang started to climb up another part of the mountain. They reached an area where there were guards.

Though these guards were doing their assignment well, they were not prepared for these two particular ninjas. Trang and Asoya took them out soundlessly and continued to climb, making their way to the top. They came across more Shin Obi halfway up. While Asoya subdued three Piranhas, a fourth one crept up behind him.

Trang just got done making a Shin Obi fall asleep by striking him on the back of the neck, quickly using his thumb and index finger; the Shin Obi fell. Trang was about sixteen feet from where Asoya was when he looked up and spotted the Shin Obi creeping up behind Asoya. Trang took out a star and launched it in Asoya's direction. The star hit the Shin Obi, who fell and did not get up again. Asoya looked behind himself and saw the Shin Obi lying on the ground; he then turned to look at Trang. Before Trang could gather himself from throwing the star, a Shin Obi crept up behind him.

"Trang! Behind you!" Asoya shouted, warning Trang about their lethal enemy.

Trang turned, "Huh?" Seeing a foot coming his way, Trang attempted to raise his arm to block it, but it was too late. The Shin Obi kicked Trang on his side. Trang lost his balance, and his arm smashed into the side of the mountain. A sharp rock that was bulging out of the side of the mountain pierced his shoulder deep, causing his shoulder to break. CRACK クラック! The noise his arm made upon breaking was chilling; it rattled, making its way into everyone's ears. Trang then stumbled over and fell; however, he doesn't fall to the ground but off the mountain.

"Trang, NO!" Asoya shouted as he ran in anger toward the Shin Obi who kicked Trang.

CHAPTER 87

AN AVALANCHE OF WELDED STEEL 雪崩

THE SHIN OBI QUICKLY TURNED AND SAW ASOYA'S focus. His focus was on him, the focus that a shark gives just before they clamp down their jaws. Asoya was not slowing down. The Shin Obi took out sharp projectiles and sent them Asoya's way. Asoya lifted his sheathed blade in front of his face as one of the metal pieces crashed into it and then fell to the ground. A second one headed his way. Asoya ducked as the metal shard went over him, and a third one followed the second.

Asoya jumped into the air as the metal flew under him. He hit the ground and rolled, then got up continuing to make his way to the Shin Obi. Asoya swung his blade, and the Shin Obi fell.

"Trang!" Asoya shouted as he made it to the edge of the cliff on the mountainside. He slid on his knees and looked down. He saw Trang hanging by just one hand, firmly gripping a stone because his other arm was damaged.

Trang looked up at Asoya and spoke. "Leave me. Complete the mission."

Asoya breathed heavily, almost in a panic. He looked back toward the mountain top, then back down at Trang.

"LEAVE!" Trang shouted, closing his eyes tightly as his voice echoed in his own ears due to Asoya's disobedience in not following a direct order.

*Orders…*Asoya thought, for he remembered the law, the laws that were made to govern assassins. Asoya arose and left as the laws and teachings of ninja mandated 命令された. The rock Trang was holding on to started to loosen. Trang closed his eyes as he started to fall. He felt a tug on his wrist. When he opened his eyes to see what it was, he saw Asoya. When Trang told Asoya to complete the mission, Asoya hurried up and set bombs in random locations around the Shin Obi's post, then tied a rope around a large rock and around his waist and jumped off the cliff, grabbing ahold of Trang's wrist.

"Trang, I got you."

"No! You are going against what we've been taught. You are NOT supposed to come back for me!"

Asoya stared at Trang with seriousness.

Trang looked down at his injured arm and then said, "You would dare go against the teachings of the clan to come back for me? Let me go, now!"

"When I was an orphan sitting alone, did you not come back for me?"

Asoya asked, prompting Trang to think. For though Asoya remembered the law, Asoya knew that the law with all of its regulated disciplines 規則 were not what got him into the clan, it was something else, something that someone did for him so that he would not perish with the rest of the villagers.

Trang looked at Asoya, frowning, but his frown slowly softened. He sighed as he thought on that day. He grinned. Asoya slowly grinned back. Trang's grin left his face because he saw multiple Shin Obi on the mountain lining up with shurikens in their hands. The metal in their hands glistened as the light of the sun touched them.

"Oh no, watch out!" Trang shouted. He shouted because Asoya did not see that they had been spotted by their enemies, and their enemies had gifts for the two intruders, their shurikens. Stars began to drop upon Trang and Asoya, 雪崩 an avalanche of welded steel.

CHAPTER 88

LACERATIONS AND EXPLOSIONS

"HANG ON!" ASOYA HOLLERED AT TRANG AS HE FIRMLY held Trang's wrist even tighter.

"Release me!" Trang demanded, seeing that Asoya was in the line of fire alone.

"No!" Asoya said with resilience as he struggled to keep his hold on Trang. "I'm not letting you go!"

A star sliced across Asoya's chest, leaving a deep and long slit on his skin. These stars were different; however, they were heated, so they did more damage.

Asoya was then hit on his side. "Arghh!" he yelled in pain, but his firm grip upon Trang still held steady. More stars scraped across his arms, forearms and abdomen.

Because of Asoya's and Trang's angle on the mountainside, it was difficult for the Shin Obi to hit them head-on. The stars grazed and skimmed across the top of Asoya's skin only to connect to the mountain wall behind them. Trang was not actually hit once.

Asoya saw a ravine below them a few feet down with enough space to stand on. Asoya looked behind himself to see how close the back of the mountain was, he then started to swing Trang back and forth. Trang looked below his feet and immediately knew what Asoya was trying to do. A star cut his forearm, the forearm he held onto Trang with, but that didn't faze Asoya. When he felt they were close enough to the mountain behind them, he released Trang.

Trang took out his blade and stuck it into the mountain. He slid, and when he stopped sliding, Trang placed both feet on the mountain wall to release his blade. He pushed off the mountain with both feet. His blade was released, so he did a backflip and then landed on the rock below them close to the ravine. Trang landed on both feet. Bending his knees, then rose slowly as he sheathed his blade. He held his broken arm then looked up at Asoya.

Asoya reached behind his back and pulled out an explosive from his pouch; another shuriken scraped across his skin, cutting his knee. He threw the explosive as hard as he could upward toward the top of the mountain where the Shin Obi's post was … BOOM! It exploded. The Shin Obi's lookout post also erupted because it was where they kept most of their explosives.

KA-BOOM カブーム!

The Shin Obi throwing the stars and the ones at the lookout post were launched back into the air from the explosion, and they slid down the other side of the mountain. Asoya swung himself to the ravine where Trang was, released himself from the rope by cutting it, and stabbed his sword into the mountainside to slow his fall, landing right next to Trang.

CHAPTER 89

NOT AN ORDINARY NINJA 剣闘士

"MISSION COMPLETE?" ASOYA ASKED, FROWNING while looking over at Trang, who, by then, had taken his eyes off the top of the mountain to look over at Asoya.

Trang frowned for a few seconds, then smiled. "Mission complete."

Asoya smiled back.

Trang and Asoya then prepared to make their descent down the mountain. Trang was unable to climb down due to his broken arm, so Asoya carried him on his back. Asoya ripped a piece of his shirt and used it to tie Trang to his back. He climbed down the mountain carrying Trang, making it to the bottom fairly quickly. Trang released himself from Asoya's back by cutting the shirt that tied him to Asoya with his shuriken, then looked up toward the top of the mountain holding his broken arm.

285

He was amazed that even though Asoya had so many cuts and scrapes on his body that were deeper than usual due to the heated metal from the Shin Obi's throwing stars, he was still able to carry him on his back down the mountain. Trang knew then that Asoya was no ordinary ninja 普通の忍者. Asoya has to be some type of natural-born combatant, a gladiator 剣闘士. He thought this because he realized that Asoya was not fatigued at all from the long descent down.

"You were cut pretty deep by multiple stars, brother. I'm going to have to heat up this dagger to burn your wounds shut so that you won't lose any more blood."

"We are sharks; these wounds are just baby bites that I sustained from fearful Piranha. We are clandestine," Asoya said as he frowned and stared in the distance. He then smiled for a second and returned his face to its serious expression.

Trang nodded his head, made a fire, and then hovered his knife over the flame until it was searing red. Asoya removed his own shirt, sat on the ground with his legs crossed and his forearms gently resting on his knees with his eyes closed. Asoya mediated, trying to divert his attention from the pain he was currently in. *Do not show your weakness*, Asoya thought, remembering the words that he was taught in the clan.

"Are you ready?" Trang asked with a hint of uneasiness in his voice, knowing that this would cause Asoya more pain and leave him permanently scarred.

"Ready," Asoya said with seriousness in his voice. The searing hot dagger did not move him. Trang began to press the hot dagger on Asoya's chest to close the wound…

The present:

Asoya comes back to reality, hearing the rumblings of thunder.

"Trang…" he says, looking back at the wall at the Ajisai flower painting. He hears the rain pounding on the ground and the trees outdoors.

CHAPTER 90

THE PLEA AND THE DRINKING OF HOT KOCHA

ASOYA TRAINS DOING PUSH-UPS TO EASE HIS MIND AS the rain continues to fall. He hears a knock at the door so he grabs ahold of his dagger as he eases to the door, not making a sound. He slowly opens the door, ready with his dagger, when lightning strikes in the background. As he raises his arm to take out the unwelcome intruder, he pauses as the lightning fades and he sees the form of who is knocking at his door.

"Elisa? How…" Asoya asks as he looks around outdoors, then quickly puts his dagger behind himself and lets Elisa in. She was drenched from the pounding rain.

"How did you find this place?" he asks as he got her a blanket and covers her with it.

"Gēto," she says, for Gēto followed Asoya in secret one day to see where he stayed, and Asoya did not know that. He lights a candle.

"I should have known it was him. And the traps I set, how did you avoid them?"

"Gēto. He showed me where those were, too. He drew me a map."

"A map?" Asoya asks trying to rationalize Gēto. "How did he know where the traps were? Only ninjas can detect such things. Smart boy, for he indeed is an intuitive one."

Elisa suddenly grabs ahold of Asoya's arm with both of her hands. He looks down at Elisa.

"Please don't go, don't leave," she says with tears in her eyes. Even though Asoya did not say it, she could tell by the look in his eyes that he was not coming back when the new orphanage was finished being built. She knows that he was ashamed for his action of drawing out his blade on the woman with the limp, Makoto.

"It's alright, Asoya. The other workers and I never held what you did against you. We prayed for you, knowing that you were going through a tough time. You were right about Makoto. She was a spy, but the Lord sent His angel and protected us from her."

Asoya sighs as he looks over at the wall, seeing Elisa's painting.

"You are always welcome at the orphanage; we need you, and the children need you. Because of you, many of the children, mainly Gēto, have gotten better and found a purpose to go on."

"Alright, alright. It's okay Elisa," he says, looking down and seeing her tears. He speaks in a calming voice, trying to stop Elisa's tears from flowing even more.

She was crying and trying to talk at the same time. She rubs her eyes, smiles as best she can and says, "Okay."

Asoya fixes Elisa some hot Kocha, also known as black tea 紅茶, to warm her up. As she drinks the tea, he reads God's word to her. She looks around as he reads, and she sees her painting hanging on the wall. She smiles upon seeing that he actually hung it up. She then sips her tea as she listens to the Word.

When she finishes drinking the tea, he walks her back to the orphanage and then heads back to his home.

CHAPTER 91

THE HIDDEN SIXTY

THERE WAS A HIDDEN REGIMENT 隠された連隊, lying in wait for Asoya. For the clan's Master sent three hundred ninjas to capture the shadow agent who broke his oaths. There were forty ninjas at the orphanage when Asoya rescued Chiasa; two hundred ninjas surrounded the abandoned house where the angel intervened. That left sixty ninjas that were unaccounted for. These sixty were reserves, just in case the two hundred and forty were not effective. Word from a messenger ninja made its way to the sixty on standby 待機する. They were equipped, so they head out, darting through the night like sharks, for they had Asoya's scent and were on his trail.

Though they were drawing closer to where Asoya was, a single shark was on the trail of the hidden agents themselves, for he was more savage than they were. This shark, this trained shadow took out all sixty, one by one, without any of them realizing what was occurring. He was noiseless, soundless, a vicious prowler. There was just one agent left pursing Asoya's scent when the masked shark tapped the hidden agent on the shoulder, and the agent turned and blew poisonous smoke through a bamboo stick at the unwelcomed guest. The smoke did nothing; the masked assassin vanished into a shadow and from this shadow, the masked assassin spoke,

"Have you forgotten that I was once the scarred assassin? What did you think was going to happen? My name is Asoya!" He shouts. As the masked assassin plunges from the shadow into the ninja, the ninja is overpowered. He looks down at the hidden agent, and he then takes off the mask he was using to veil his identity. After all, the masked assassin was not Asoya but a ruse; it was actually the Red Velvet Shuriken, Trang. The clan has no knowledge of Trang's presence, for he was there without permission from the clan's Master the entire time.

Trang had secretly left his undercover assignment in the Northern quadrant of Japan to see if what was spoken about Asoya was true. During Asoya's entire encounter with Trang, no ninjas from the clan knew of Trangs's presence; he was concealed, clandestine 秘密の, a true ninja. Trang made it seem as though Asoya was the one who took out all sixty agents to buy Asoya some time. He makes a new trail leading the clan away from Asoya's current location and making it seem that he had fled to another nation, India.

CHAPTER 92

AVERTED SCHEME

THIS IS THE LAW 法律 AND OATH OF AN ASSASSIN: remain in the clan's shadow; just like a shark must remain in the water to survive, an assassin must remain in the shadows. Ninjas make oaths to their clan, and to the clan, those oaths must be kept. Trang was one who followed his oaths to the utmost. He was not ordered to do anything he did against Asoya; he did it in secret. Only Trang and a messenger spy knew that he tracked down Asoya. It started out with him seeking his shadow brother, but it turned into a vendetta ヴェンデッタ after he saw that that his brother broke the rule of ninja, and that rule was not to forget that once one has bathed in the shadows, they must remain in it.

After looking at a handful of the sixty ninjas on the ground, Trang ties a scroll to one of the ninja's sheaths as he saw Asoya do numerous times. He takes off like a missile soaring through the evening shadows, making a trail for the clan to follow. He frowns as he tries to rationalize the words on the scroll that he tied to the ninja's sheath; the contents of the scroll speak of where Jesus proclaimed in John 8:24, "I said therefore unto you, that you shall die in your sins: for if you believe not that I am he (the promised One to come that the prophets spoke about, the Savior of all people, the bearer of everyone's sins, the Messiah), you shall die in your sins."

"Sins…" Trang repeats as he ran several miles. He stops running, turns and looks back, and catches his breath. As he turns back around and looks up, he discovers that he is at the foot of a mountain and on the other side of the mountain is a flowing riverbank that leads into the ocean. He climbs using various tools that he has in his arsenal. After forty-five minutes of climbing, he makes it to the top, and although it was night, at that height, the land could be surveyed from many angles. The scenery was something that even Trang marveled at; the land of Japan was beautiful. The wind and air are different at this height and elevation; it has a certain coolness, so he sits down on top of one of the large stones to watch the shy. There was flashing but no noise.

"I've hidden myself and listened to the way others have spoken of you since you left the clan. They use such terms as kindness to describe your character and actions. I've also heard of you being a giver and a helper to those who are weak. At first, I thought you were playing a game, some charade, but this was no game."

The wind blows hard, but only for a minute. Trang pulls out a scroll that Asoya left for him and opens it, reading out loud, "Jesus said in this scroll that I read in John 8:30 and 8:36, to those who believe in Him, for them to continue in His Word and those who stay and remain in His Word are His disciples (students, followers). Those are the ones who will know the truth, and the truth shall make them free."

Trang moves his fingers over the words he just read, and places his finger on one word…free.

"You were looking for freedom, and it seems you have found it. Not freedom from the clan but within, freedom from sin 罪業, and the stains that sin carries with it," Trang says, rolling up the scroll and putting it on his side. He then eases his blade from its case, and looks down at the steel, feeling the weight of his own sins.

"Sins," he says, and as he spins his sword and points it at the trees below him, he slowly lowers it.

"Everyone on this earth is looking for something, and you found what you have always been looking for, brother, something that the clan or I could not give you, forgiveness. Forgiveness for your sins and a place that you belong, and that place is in the Kingdom that Jesus resides in."

Trang pushes his blade into its sheath and ties it to his back. He looks at the scar on his shoulder that he sustained on a mission and how Asoya went against what the clan taught to save him from falling.

He chuckles to himself. "You never really belonged in the clan, I've always known this. For a time, you became Vermillion, but even as Vermillion, this Jesus somehow found His way to your heart. He has not relinquished His hold on you and you have not given up your hold on Him. I've tried many times to get you to lay your hold back on the clan, but you have refused. Though I did see you struggle, despite the struggle, you got back up. I guess that's the gladiator side of you."

He smiles. Two miles back, Piranhas were on the move. They caught Trang's trail and are pursuing him; these Piranhas are the Shin Obi.

"It is because of this and your unyielding belief in this Master you are now following that I have averted my scheme and pursuit of you."

The Piranhas draw closer as the sky continues to flash its vibrant light.

CHAPTER 93

THE PIRANHAS

TRANG LOWERS THE THIN VEIL THAT COVERS HIS NOSE and mouth and pulls back the hood from over his head. His hair moves with the wind, and he closes his eyes as the sky continues to soundlessly flash its light.

"I witnessed something I have never seen before—power arising from a scroll, and this power surrounded you! A mystery to me; it was protection. Upon further reconnaissance and information gathering, it was revealed to me that the power was not in the scrolls themselves but in the belief in the One you serve who empowers you, your Masutā, your Master … Jesus."

He opens his eyes. Shin Obi appear like a mist and surround the mountain below, for they are piranhas ピラニア and knew that there was a change in the water. A shark had swum somewhere he was not supposed to swim, and they were coming for him. The sky flashed.

"There is no argument from what I read myself, 良いマスター Jesus is a good Masutā, a Master I would have liked to have had followed before I made unbreakable vows to the clan. I see why you follow Him," says Trang.

The Shin Obi climb as though they were drifting in the sea; their movements as they climb were unnerving and eerie. Though their movements were random, not one rock shifted or moved. The piranhas make it to the top of the mountain where the shark was seated, fifty in all. Trang was in enemy territory and knew it, but he did not care. He knew that his enemies surfaced the moment they started climbing. He lifts the black silk-like cloth that was around his neck, covering his nose and mouth. Trang then grins hard, so hard that his eyes smile.

He takes out eight regular throwing stars, four in each hand. He remains seated, calmly and coolly unalarmed. Asoya was ruthless when dealing with his enemies in the past, but Trang, Trang's demeanor was something else entirely, and his combating skills could be considered *ballistic*, berserk 凶暴な.

During Asoya and Trang's battle against each other, Trang was holding back, not even unleashing half of the moves he learned from other styles when fighting Asoya, and Asoya was well aware of this. Lighting strikes, revealing all fifty Shin Obi's locations atop the mountain, so Trang lifts his head, laughs, and says upon seeing their drawn weapons pointed at him. "Have any of you heard about a shark that was once called the Megalodon?"

The Shin Obis did not reply; they only eased in closer to Trang, still pointing their razor-sharp blades at him.

"There are many tales spoken about this massive shark, for it was the largest of all the sharks and is said from history to have existed thousands of years ago. It was not just the largest but also the most deadly! I am the Megalodon," he says, then he starts to laugh in a whisper-like manner. After a few moments, he frowns, looking up at the Piranhas before him.

"I am hungry. And to my surprise, LOOK what the ocean has washed ashore, and brushed ever so benevolently before me, to be digested as food! Every single one of you will be eaten…a mauling has befallen you. But before you all are consumed, I will leave you with these three words…" he says, showing the Shin Obi eight of his throwing stars.

"Beware — my shurikens."

Lighting strikes, making a loud crashing sound that shakes the top of the mountain. The entire sky lights up, but when the light went away, Trang was no longer seated on the rock but was behind one of the Piranhas. None of them saw him move. Trang did what sharks do when they are around food; he swallows his enemies whole. Not one was able to stand against the kismet of his berserk attacks 凶暴な攻撃, not one.

CHAPTER 94

THE QUESTION

TRANG LOOKS DOWN AT HIS FISTS, THE MEGALODON'S fists, that just dropped all fifty Shin Obis with ease. He then opens both hands as he thought about Asoya no longer being a hitman but a Word Carrier.

"You're not a shark any longer; do not attempt to swim in these waters, the waters of assassins. You don't belong here, despite me wanting you to return," Trang says lowering the hood that was over his head. Trang did not kill any of his enemies but made it seem like Asoya took them out without using lethal force due to that route being the quickest to sail to India. The Piranhas are unconscious.

"Do not return to the shadows again, brother," Trang says as he runs close to the cliffs edge, then jumps off, descending downwards and plummeting into the water below.

Splash スプラッシュ！

301

Once he resurfaces from under the water, he swims over to where a small boat was located that was close to the dock; he takes the boat and sails to India. The next day, Asoya prepares to go on a month's journey to a certain city in Japan, but he decides to head to the new orphanage to see the children before he leaves.

When he arrives, he sees someone out front raking leaves. It was Chiasa, and she has a smile on her face and this smile is due to everyone returning safely. *The Lord truly delivers His people, He delivers those who trust in Him*, she thinks as she rakes.

Asoya walks up to her slowly. He has a look like that of a child that has gotten in trouble and is ashamed. Chiasa stops raking when she sees that Asoya has arrived. She walks over to him with haste, tears fill her eyes, and she grabs him gently by the hand and pats it softly. Asoya looks down at her.

"I see that the Omnipotent One has kept you safe, too, for the shadow that you have chosen to follow is His and not the shadow that has come from your past. I am very glad. Welcome back, Word Carrier."

Chiasa squeezes his hand as a mother would her son, then walks over to the rake, picks it up, and continues her raking with a smile. "The Word Carrier made it back safely, all praises to Him who dwells on high," she said as she starts to hum a song.

Asoya goes past her with a smile on his face as well and walks up the wooden stairs. When he made it up the five steps, he knocks on the front door. The door slides open as one of the workers greets him at the door and lets him in with a smile, for she, too, was happy that he was safe. Gēto greets him as well once he realizes Asoya has arrived, bowing before him to show respect.

"Do you mind putting this against the wall?" Asoya asks as he extends his sheathed blade towards Gēto.

Grinning, Gēto grabs hold of it with both hands, "Yes, Master Asoya."

"What did I tell you about calling me that?"

"I know ..." Gēto says, running off to put the sword against the wall.

"But you're still my Master!" he says, sprinting to sit down where the other children were. Asoya walks over to the group of children and sits down as he opens a scroll and starts to read to them Psalm 91:1."He who dwells in the secret place of the Most High shall abide under the shadow of the Almighty."

"Master Asoya, what is the shadow of the Almighty?" Gēto asks.

"It's His protection."

"Oh ... his protection, that's very cool," Gēto says understanding the concept 概念.

"We were protected because we dwelt in the Lord," one of the children says, knowing that God's protection was very real.

"That's right," Elisa says with happiness as Asoya continues to read from Psalm 91:2.

"I will say of the LORD, He is my refuge and my fortress: my God; in him will I trust."

He pauses, then starts to think and says out loud, "O Most High, I abide under Your shadow. I trust in You and not my own sword," while looking over at his sword leaning against the wall.

"Mr. Asoya ..." the young girl named Laughter says, giggling, "You're doing it again."

"Ah, yes, my apologies," Asoya says, looking back over at the children and giving them his attention once more.

"It's okay," the little one named Smiles says, excited to listen to more of Asoya's words.

"This is what David said of the Lord because he had a personal relationship with God, and you can have one with Him, too. This is the question from Psalm 91:2: what do you say of the Lord?"

CHAPTER 95

THE ART OF STILLNESS 静けさの芸術

THE ART OF STILLNESS DOES NOT MEAN A PERSON does not do anything at all, but rather it means that they humble themselves enough as they go throughout their day to think, remember and understand that God is God in every situation. They understand that even though there are those who do not serve Him or believe in Him, God is still God and will be exalted high above them all, not just above them but above every living thing, for He is El Elyon אל עליון the Most High God, and despite the things that occur upon the earth, God will still be exalted by those who trust in Him on the earth as long as they live. Those who trust in Him abide under His shadow. This is what Word Carriers do, and this is the true art of stillness 静止.

End of *Asoya*: **Shadows From the Past:**

Trang (忍者、ヒットマン)

信頼
Trust

Psalms 34:17, 2 Samuel 22:4

For they got not the land in possession by their own sword, neither did their own arm save them: but your right hand, and your arm, and the light of your countenance, because you hadst a favour unto them.

(Psalms 44:3)

For I will not trust in my bow,
neither shall my sword save me. But
you have saved us from our enemies, and have
put them to shame that hated us.
(Psalms 44:6-7)

全能の影

The Almighty/Omnipotent Ones Shadow

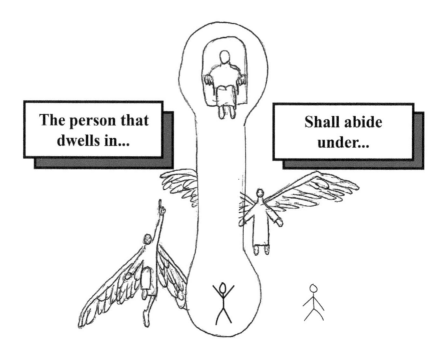

The person that dwells in...

Shall abide under...

The person that chooses to dwell in the Lord
shall/*will* abide under His shadow (*His protection*).
This person has a refuge, a fortress, deliverance,
covering, shielding, comfort
from fear so they are not afraid. He *commands*
his angels to protect them.
(Psalm 91:1-12)

MORE STORIES

AVAILABLE SOON FROM JOSEPH DAVAULIA

Asoya; From Darkness to Light

Asoya; Shadows From the Past: Part 1 *Vermillion*
(The Rewrite And Reprint Available 2022)

Asoya; The Scarred Ninja and Katana

Asoya; Uninitiated Affiliations

Asoya; Uninitiated Affiliations *Part 2* The Ninja and the Samurai

Hatogi; The Japanese Ancient

Geto; Blessed Are the Peacemakers

Asoya; Hostilities Of The Adversary

B.F.O.B.F.; Goshen the Warrior

B.F.O.B.F.; Salvation Over Spinning Funnels

B.F.O.B.F.; The Fiery Darts of the Wicked One

B.F.O.B.F.; Sweet Tea yea!

B.F.O.B.F.; Love Your Enemies

P.V.; The Land Where Anything Goes

P.V.; Flaming Union

Parch'er Then a Desert

Flares Amidst Shadows ™

Matthew 5:15-16

煌々

Praise God
Win Souls
Blaze Brightly

Psalms 46:10

赤　影

Be still, and know that I am God:
I will be exalted among the heathen, I will
be exalted in the earth.

CPSIA information can be obtained
at www.ICGtesting.com
Printed in the USA
BVHW050846071221
623415BV00022B/990